The Unauthorized Trek

DEEP SPACE

The Voyage Continues

James Van Hise
Hal Schuster

PIONEER BOOKS INC

Recently Released Pioneer Books. . .

TO ORDER CALL TOLL FREE: (800)444-2524 ext. 67
credit cards happily accepted

Library of Congress Cataloging-in-Publication Data
James Van Hise, 1959—
Hal Schuster, 1955—

The Unauthorized Trek: Deep Space The Voyage Continues

1.   The Unauthorized Trek: Deep Space The Voyage Continues

(television, popular culture)
I. Title

Published by Pioneer Books, Inc., 5715 N. Balsam Rd., Las Vegas, NV, 89130.

First Printing, 1994

PUBLISHER, EDITOR, DESIGNER: Hal Schuster
COVER ART BY Bruce Wood, COVER DESIGN BY Hal Schuster
All interior photographs c 1994 Albert L. Ortega

TABLE OF CONTENTS

The Unauthorized Trek

DEEP SPACE

The Voyage Continues

WITHER DEEP SPACE?

It seems like just yesterday that this new STAR TREK spin-off began. Now it is the end of the second season.

DEEP SPACE NINE was more readily accepted by viewers and critics in January 1993 than STAR TREK—THE NEXT GENERATION was when it began in 1987. The question of "Can they do this again?" wasn't there. We knew they could do it again. Rather we were interested in seeing a new approach to STAR TREK.

The characters were compared to those on previous STAR TREK series because they fit certain types: The commander. The doctor. An unhuman alien.

Odo is to DEEP SPACE NINE what Data is to THE NEXT GENERATION and Spock is to the original STAR TREK. They are all similar yet different.

The rumors of "darker" stories and characters proved false. The main characters on DEEP SPACE NINE are honest and upstanding.

Even Major Kira, a former Bajoran terrorist, condemned the tactics of her comrades and repudiated the movement. Had Kira been unapologetic about her past, her character would have had more dimension.

STAR TREK heroes must be squeaky clean. Even Quark is shown to be generous, humane and un-Ferengi in acts of kindness.

These are not the characters of novels. They are TV heroes. No darkness here.

The characters were quickly scrubbed clean. Commander Sisko initially hated Captain Picard because of his involvement with the Borg at the time Jennifer Sisko was killed. All of Ben's emotional problems on this were resolved in the first episode! No lingering pain. No sleepless nights. Put the past behind us and move on, as impossible as that may be for people in real life.

Major Kira initially disliked and distrusted Sisko and the Federation. Those misgivings disappeared within a couple of episodes.

Clashes between characters are infrequent and inconsequential. They seem larger on DEEP SPACE NINE because THE NEXT GENERATION command crew acted as if they were all on Valium.

DEEP SPACE NINE may be too cozy and sedate. The producers recognized it. Late in season two they added the Maquis. Then the villainous Vedek Winn became Kai and the Dominion joined the mix. They are the biggest threat to face the Federation since the Borg!

The Borg tried to invade the Federation. The Dominion drew a line in the sand and dared the Federation to cross it after destroying a starship and wiping out a Bajoran colony in the Gamma Quadrant.

The Dominion blockaded the wormhole. Instead of a promise of the future it now represents a threat. It casts a shadow over storylines. You cannot conduct business as usual when a powerful threat lurks minutes away.

The third season of DEEP SPACE NINE is set for real fireworks from three possible directions. All have the potential to worsen existing situations.

The final frontier has just taken on a whole new meaning.

—James Van Hise

DEEP SPACE

The Background

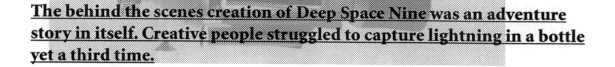

The behind the scenes creation of Deep Space Nine was an adventure story in itself. Creative people struggled to capture lightning in a bottle yet a third time.

CREATION

January 1993 marked the launch of STAR TREK: DEEP SPACE NINE. Ironically the announcement of the plans to produce this series came shortly after the death of Gene Roddenberry in late 1991. The timing led to speculation that had Roddenberry lived, this series might not have. Suspicions along these lines were raised particularly after descriptions of this new series filtered out. "It's going to be darker and grittier than THE NEXT GENERATION," executive producer Rick Berman stated in the March 6, 1992 ENTERTAINMENT WEEKLY. "The characters won't be squeaky clean."

To the fans, STAR TREK has always meant just that—squeaky clean heroes. What would Gene Roddenberry have thought of this? After all, people close to him have stated that Gene hated STAR TREK VI merely because it postulated Enterprise crew members who were anti-Klingon bigots. In the future that Roddenberry made, humankind had outgrown such pettiness. Gene overlooked the fact that in the 1966 STAR TREK episode "Balance of Terror," an Enterprise crewman was postulated as being an angry anti-Romulan bigot who transferred his feelings of mistrust and suspicion to Mr. Spock when it was discovered that Romulans and Vulcans were of the same race. As it has turned out, though, the only character on the new series who has a real dark side is Quark. Major Kira is a former terrorist, but she fought on the correct side of the conflict. At worst, Dax had an affair with a married woman when the Trill was in her former host body, that of the man Curzon Dax. The characters couldn't be much more well-scrubbed than this.

Rick Berman and Michael Piller were originally at a loss for a title for the newest addition to the STAR TREK canon. They toyed with calling the series "The Final Frontier" and having the space station re-christened with a Starbase number after the Federation took over the day-to-day operations of the station. Having a series with a Cardassian or Bajoran name was not considered a terribly good marketing ploy. In the course of the series' development, the station was dubbed "Deep Space Nine," a temporary appellation which not only became permanent but which also became the title for the fledgling series itself, despite Piller and Berman's dissatisfaction with the name.

Even though the announcement about DEEP SPACE NINE seemed to come from out of nowhere several weeks after Roddenberry's death, Michael Piller and Rick Berman had actually been discussing ideas for a new series for some time. It was always planned to be a spin-off from STAR TREK. Even though the ideas were discussed with Paramount, it never went beyond the planning stages. When Brandon Tarticoff moved from being the head of NBC to being the head of Paramount, he told Rick Berman that he wanted to see a spin-off from STAR TREK to launch into syndication. Berman and Pillar returned to their series notes and worked up a proposal for DEEP SPACE NINE.

The reason that Paramount wanted a new STAR TREK television series to run concurrent with THE NEXT GENERATION is to help establish DEEP SPACE NINE so that when THE NEXT GENERATION goes into reruns, a new and different STAR TREK series will already have been established and be in place in the syndication market. STAR TREK: DEEP SPACE NINE is being syndicated with another new Paramount series, a revival of the fifties series THE UNTOUCHABLES. The ratings success of DEEP SPACE NINE, which has put it neck and neck with THE NEXT GENERATION, has thus far shown Paramount's judgment in launching the new series to be a sound one.

RODDENBERRY INFLUENCE

Rick Berman insists that DEEP SPACE NINE is not going to be his and executive producer Michael Piller's own personal take on STAR TREK. He states that this series is just another way of expressing Gene Roddenberry's vision and it is fitting and consistent with everything that has been done with STAR TREK before. DEEP SPACE NINE was initially announced as having been developed under Gene's guidance and with his input. However later statements contradicted this and indicated that while STAR TREK's creator was aware of the plans for DEEP SPACE NINE, he wasn't directly involved with it at any time.

Regarding Roddenberry's influence on DEEP SPACE NINE, Piller explained, "Every writer knows that we have a responsibility to maintain his vision. We take it very seriously. I got a letter from twenty-five grade school children, and the teacher, who said, 'Please, we use STAR TREK as an example of life in the future and the optimistic view and the hope that Gene gave us. We've heard that this is going to be dark and dreary.' And the truth is that it is not."

But by the time Roddenberry created the backdrop for THE NEXT GENERATION, he had adopted the philosophy that all the members of Starfleet should be in harmony, particularly those who work together on a starship. "He had very clear-cut rules about Starfleet officers having any tension or conflict between themselves. His futuristic humans were too good for that," Berman told VARIETY in the January 25, 1993 issue. "As a result, it's very difficult to write for these people, because out of conflict comes good drama."

Producer Rick Berman sees the show as a means of escaping the somewhat limiting constraints of Gene Roddenberry's original STAR TREK concept. "We set about creating a situation, an environment, and a group of characters that could have conflict without breaking Gene's rules. We took our characters and placed them in an unfamiliar environment, one that lacked the state-of-the-art comfort of the Enterprise, and where there were people who didn't want them there."

On Deep Space Nine, set in a rough and tumble corner of the known universe, Berman sees a lot more room for conflict. "By putting Starfleet characters on an alien space station with alien creatures, you have immediate conflicts.

"The truth is that there is more conflict," Pillar says, trying to put the show and its various elements into perspective, "that we're in a part of the universe that is giving us more conflict. And the fact that we are on an alien space station instead of the Enterprise will allow us to do that. But it is the same Gene Roddenberry optimism for the future of mankind that drives the vision of this show. There is not going to be any more

CREATION

shooting, more weapons or battles or anything like that. Certainly we're going to have action. It's going to be an adventure show and it's an entertainment show. We wanted to find the camaraderie that existed in the original STAR TREK, like that relationship between McCoy and Spock, and in order to do that you have to have differences, and differences between the characters on THE NEXT GENERATION are not so clearly defined."

One character whose personality is explored more is Miles O'Brien. He has more room to be curt and unpleasant from time to time. Less regimented than a Federation ship, the space station from which DEEP SPACE NINE draws its title, leaves its inhabitants more room to express the less agreeable aspects of their personalities from time to time. On the other hand, this also leads to scenes in which O'Brien and Commander Sisko discuss matters in a considerably more relaxed and informal fashion than O'Brien would ever have been able to employ while speaking with Captain Picard.

"There are characters who come through much darker than the NEXT GENERATION characters, but I don't know that I could say this is a dark series," Piller says reflectively. "It's still Gene Roddenberry's vision. It has an optimistic view of mankind in the future. Reason and dialog and communication are still the key weapons in the fight to solve problems. I think the label of darker is probably exaggerated."

A NEW ORDER

Michael Piller never had any doubt that there was room for a third STAR TREK series. He feels that Gene Roddenberry created a huge universe of characters and concepts. "Gene used to say, somewhat in kidding, but in a way to communicate what he wanted to do with STAR TREK, that space was like the old west, and that STAR TREK was like WAGON TRAIN. In that whole genre of the west there were dozens of television shows. In the universe that Gene has created there is room, not only for a WAGON TRAIN, but also for a GUNSMOKE. In essence, what I think we're doing is the counterpart to the kind of shows you saw on the old west where you have a Ft. Sheridan on the edge of the frontier, and a frontier town in a very active area with a lot of people coming through it."

Among the other ideas Berman and Piller discussed was the concept of creating a sort of futuristic Hong Kong on a planet surface and building a set in the desert north of Los Angeles where they'd film the series.

"We felt that would be extremely expensive and difficult to produce," Piller stated in VARIETY, "so we took our Hong Kong and put it on a space station, then we scaled it back in order to make it cost-effective."

Berman explained that coming up with DEEP SPACE NINE after working on THE NEXT GENERATION was like living in a house for several years and then deciding to remodel.

"This was how we felt about STAR TREK. It was very close to us, but there was a lot of 'wouldn't it be nice.' Developing DEEP SPACE NINE gave us the opportunity to rebuild the house."

The groundwork for STAR TREK: DEEP SPACE NINE was created in a couple of episodes of THE NEXT GENERATION: "Ensign Ro" and "The Wounded." Viewers met their first Bajoran in the person of the troublesome Ensign Ro (portrayed by Michele Forbes), and got a glimpse of the difficult conditions on Bajor after a century of occupation by the genuinely disagreeable Cardassians. Just prior to the premiere of DEEP SPACE NINE, THE NEXT GENERATION featured a two-part episode in which Captain Picard was captured and tortured by Cardassians.

But it seems that much of what would lead to the ideas for DEEP SPACE NINE grew out of the political situation that was created for the fifth season NEXT GENERATION episode "Ensign Ro."

"We did not create Ensign Ro as a potential spin-off, but for all intents and purposes, that's where the tableau was set for this. We had intended to bring that character with us to DEEP SPACE NINE," Michael Piller explained on the QVC cable channel during his appearance there Dec. 5, 1992, "but the actress, who we love, Michelle Forbes, simply wasn't interested in doing a series. So after we had actually written a bible and created a script, we had to write that character out of it. But it all grew out of that character." A different actor, Nana Visitor, was cast in the role of the Bajoran regular on the series, Major Kira Nerys. She is Benjamin Sisko's first officer and the station's Bajoran attaché, and of her role she states, "The thing that is the most excit-

Bajor has been described as a stripped mining planet, but one whose culture is very conscious of the spiritual and the mystical. The Bajorans even believe that the stationary wormhole was created through divine intervention. Its existence has saved what was a dying, backwater world. One of the semi-regular characters is a religious leader from Bajor who holds very strong views on the purpose of the wormhole, although this aspect has not yet been played up. In fact the Kai has appeared only in "The Emissary" and has not had any important impact on the first ten episodes beyond that initial appearance. Named Kai Opaka, the series bible indicates that she is to be a semi-regular and provides a fairly adequate description of her. She is the spiritual leader of Bajor who is intended to provide a sharp counterpoint to the secular nature of Starfleet. The Kai can supposedly explore her guests' 'pagh' (which refers to a person's energy meridian) through deep tissue massage of their ears and this can supposedly reveal a person's true nature. I expect Quark would particularly enjoy this encounter.

In the premiere episode, it is the Kai who reveals to Sisko that he's fated to find the celestial temple, the source of the mysterious and wondrous orbs which are a vital element of the Bajoran religion. According to the DEEP SPACE NINE series bible, "The Kai seems to have an awareness on a higher plane of consciousness, and knows things she cannot possibly know. Although our people do not accept her 'powers' at face value, we cannot always explain them either. She speaks in vague, mystical and indirect language, forcing the listener to seek her meaning."

PITCHING THE SPIN-OFF

These two veterans of STAR TREK: THE NEXT GENERATION had been thinking about creating a new series together for some time. It was Rick Berman, in fact, who first presented Gene Roddenberry with the notion of a NEXT GENERATION spin-off. But Roddenberry died in October of 1991, before he and Berman could discuss the idea at any length. In a famous meeting with Tartikoff and studio executive John Pike, Rick Berman revealed that, by a happy coincidence, he and Michael Piller already had a series concept in the works. Actually, they

ing is the script, and the fact that the women in the show are very strong, very powerful, and that it's a lot to do with what's going on in the world right now." Kira Nerys is portrayed as a strong action hero of the kind who would even lead rescue missions.

Berman and Piller wrote several different versions of the series bible while it was being developed. When they finally showed a later version to Paramount, the studio provided its own input into the project, and in fact Brandon Tarticoff (before he left Paramount) suggested that the show might be something like THE RIFLEMAN in outer space, although Berman and Piller didn't quite feel that this idea particularly fit in with what they were trying to develop. But the studio's suggestions were weighed and incorporated into the series concept to produce the final result used now. In fact the father and son idea that Brandon Tarticoff was talking about did appeal to Berman and Piller and that element is very much a part of the series. The series bible is called that because it serves as the basis of development for the entire series. All of the characters and their relationships are outlined in it as well as the background of everything used in the series.

The space station itself, often referred to simply as "DS9," was itself built by the Cardassians, to serve, among other things, as an orbiting watch tower over their unruly colony. When Commander Sisko finally comes to the station, however, he finds that it has been largely gutted by the departing imperialists.

BAJOR: A PLANET ABUSED

The space station, Deep Space Nine, was established by the Cardassians and the Bajorans in conjunction with other alien races. As a result it reflects cultural needs and biases often unfamiliar to some Starfleet personnel. The station was considered of remote interest until the first fixed, stationary wormhole was discovered near the star system where Bajor is located. In fact this wasn't discovered until after Commander Sisko was posted to the space station. This discovery, in fact, caused the Cardassians to consider retaking Deep Space Nine and Bajor for its strategic importance.

had more than one: another, non-STAR TREK concept involved a series with a mediaeval setting for its science fiction plots. This was a handy alternative in case Piller and Berman were unable to sway the Paramount studio from its reluctance to do a spin-off of THE NEXT GENERATION.

It was back in October of 1991, when Piller and Berman began developing the show, that they decided to set the series in the same time frame as THE NEXT GENERATION. "That was a decision made consciously to take advantage of all of the alien races; the universe that has been developed over the last five years of THE NEXT GENERATION. We have characters we want to bring onto DEEP SPACE NINE that we've seen on THE NEXT GENERA-TION. We've got political situations. We've got relationships with the Romulans and the Klingons, and most of all, of course, the Cardassians."

When approval for the spin-off was handed down, the team of Berman and Piller had already done plenty of work on the concept, but now the time had come to really knuckle down. It wasn't as if they had a lot of spare time, either; both men were still actively involved in their respective jobs on STAR TREK: THE NEXT GENERATION, then in its fifth season. In addition to developing DEEP SPACE NINE and writing the pilot, they had to keep working on STAR TREK: THE NEXT GENERATION as well.

Rick Berman is the absolute boss on STAR TREK: THE NEXT GEN-ERATION in the wake of Gene Roddenberry's passing. On DEEP SPACE NINE, he shares the helm with Michael Piller.

Rick Berman and Michael Piller are both veterans of THE NEXT GENERATION and Piller came on board following experiences writing on staff for the television series SIMON AND SIMON and MIAMI VICE. Piller got involved in television as a journalist. He began in CBS Hollywood checking the accuracy of docudramas. His ambition was to become a producer to protect what he wrote because of all the rewriting which is done to television scripts. Piller had also previously worked on the short-lived science fiction series HARD TIME ON PLANET EARTH.

Michael Piller's job as executive producer of DEEP SPACE NINE primarily involves overseeing the writing and development of ideas for the series. In this capacity he oversees the staff writers and works with the writer of each and every script. Rick Berman participates in that somewhat while he also contributes to Berman's specialty, which is overseeing the production, editing, post-production, music and other aspects of producing the series.

DEEP SPACE NINE producer Michael Piller began his association with the STAR TREK universe when he took charge of the scripting staff for STAR TREK: THE NEXT GENERATION during the third season. He became acquainted with producer Maurice Hurley who invited him to meet with Gene Roddenberry. This led to an episode assignment on THE NEXT GENERATION. Shortly after, Hurley left THE NEXT GENERATION and Piller was invited to join the production staff. "For the next year or so," said Piller, "Gene was really on my case and certainly Rick was on my case. Day after day, we went through the creative process as I began to learn to see life through Gene Roddenberry's eyes. And even as he became sick and trusted Rick and I more and more to execute this vision, to this day, even in death, he is an extraordinary influence on both of us." He is generally credited with being responsible for the subsequent changes in NEXT GENERATION story development as well as general script improvement. When the shift over to DEEP SPACE NINE came, one of Piller's first tasks was to hire Ira Behr as one of his main writers; he hired Peter Allan Fields away from THE NEXT GENERATION to write as well.

With the advent of the new series, Piller has bowed out of some of his NEXT GENERATION tasks but still maintains control over script development along with executive producer Jeri Taylor. His main focus was on his new project: his goal for DEEP SPACE NINE was to oversee the production of eighteen scripts for the first, short season.

WRITING EMISSARY

Piller admits that he was influenced slightly by the NEXT GENERATION pilot, "Encounter at Farpoint," for the DEEP SPACE NINE pilot, "Emissary." Piller took his cue from "Encounter At Farpoint" in delaying the introduction of some key characters until later in the story. (Geordi and Riker only came in much later in the NEXT GENERATION pilot, for instance.)

"Emissary," scripted by Piller from a story by Berman and Piller, would cost as high as twelve million dollars to film (two million of which went to building the standing sets for the series). Obviously, Paramount was more than willing to bank on this project.

Another key plot ingredient inspired by "Encounter At Farpoint" was the necessity of having the lead character (in this case, Benjamin Sisko) explain or justify humanity to an alien race. This may already have become a bit of a cliché in the STAR TREK universe. How many times did Jim Kirk face the same basic problem during his career? It must have run a close second to outsmarting malevolent computers. This time around Piller managed to be give the idea an interesting spin. Sisko must communicate with aliens who do not understand humans and their ilk because they do not, themselves, experience time in a linear fashion (if at all). Sisko is thus faced with the difficult task of explaining time, human consciousness, and the importance of humanity's past experiences to an utterly uncomprehending alien form of consciousness. (One might suspect that these aliens were in fact Kurt Vonnegut's Tralfamadorians out on a lark, but no evidence to support this idea can be found in the pilot as filmed, alas.)

Unfortunately, Piller was dissatisfied with his early versions of the script for "Emissary," and continually involved a somewhat reluctant Rick Berman in constant rehashing of their original story ideas. The basic plot with Sisko explaining humanity to the unseen aliens was, Piller thought, too talky (which brought THE NEXT GENERATION episode "Unification II" to Piller's mind!), and the other aspect of the story— the transition to Federation command of the space station— seemed to be suffering.

In the early concepts of the series, the setting of DEEP SPACE NINE was to have been a dilapidated, seedy space station with technology that lagged somewhat behind that of the Federation. In the course of series development, this notion had been scrapped in favor of a more high-tech look. Now, however, Piller was forced to re-think his whole approach.

The Los Angeles riots of 1992 gave Piller his breakthrough idea. While the station would still be a fairly advanced piece of alien technology, Piller decided that the departing Cardassians would ransack the place, leaving a shambles that Sisko would be faced with rebuilding. Now the new commander's job would involve convincing the merchants of the Promenade, and other inhabitants of the station, to stay and pull things back together.

This, in turn, helped Piller to develop the relationship between Security Chief Odo (Rene Auberjonois) and the Ferengi huckster Quark (Armin Shimerman).

BERMAN AND ZIMMERMAN

Rick Berman is quick to insist that the creation of DEEP SPACE NINE has in no way diminished the quality of STAR TREK: THE NEXT GENERATION. Claiming the sixth season of THE NEXT GENERATION as one of the best yet.

Ignoring the theory, expounded by certain cynics, that THE NEXT GENERATION is being made worse intentionally in order to draw bored fans' attention to DEEP SPACE NINE, Berman is hopeful that both series will claim a sizable audience, pointing out that there are considerable differences between the two series. DEEP SPACE NINE is not, after all, a carbon copy of THE NEXT GENERATION.

Herman Zimmerman comes to DEEP SPACE NINE with a strong STAR TREK background: after all, he designed the first season for STAR TREK: THE NEXT GENERATION, as well as working on the feature films STAR TREK V: THE FINAL FRONTIER and STAR TREK VI: THE UNDISCOVERED COUNTRY. After five years away from television, he responded eagerly when Berman asked him to work on the set design for the new series.

Sets for "Emissary" cost more than those for STAR TREK VI: THE UNDISCOVERED COUNTRY: a whopping two million dollars! And under Zimmerman's guidance, the DEEP SPACE NINE sets were created from scratch. This was, after all, to be a new setting for a series. With no reference point for Cardassian architecture, it was necessary for Zimmerman and his team to invent it out of thin air.

In designing the Cardassian architecture, Zimmerman was inspired by the Cardassian look already established on THE NEXT GENERATION. Unfortunately, even this was limited, as the interior of the Cardassian ships had never been seen. So Zimmerman drew primarily from Bob Blackman's design for Cardassian costuming, an armored look was that somewhat crustacean in appearance. Part of the theory was that the Cardassians were big on structure, and if Cardassians felt structure was of vital importance, they would (like a crab, Zimmerman reasoned) keep structures on the outside. Zimmerman visualized a space station whose basic framework was not concealed inside, as in human architecture, but one where all supports and structures were clearly visible both inside the sets and with outside views of the entire station.

CREATION

Working with Zimmerman's basic concept, Nathan Cowley and Joe Hodges melded the desired crustacean concept with the heavy-handed impressiveness of Fascist architecture for the show's sets. As finally realized, the sets are quite imposing, but they still have their own unique appeal, a strangely alien sort of streamlining. Cardassian Post-modernism if you will.

As the Cardassians are very military, their Command/Ops center (which combines all the features of Transporter room, engineering and command functions in one central location) was placed by Zimmerman in such a fashion that the commander's office can look down on it and see everything that is going on. There are literally windows everywhere in that office, so that the Cardassian commander would have had no blind spots whatsoever. The Cardassians commander's staff must have been very uncomfortable indeed under his watchful gaze.

A HOSTILE ENVIRONMENT

Part of Zimmerman's design concept was that the sets and devices on the Cardassian-built station were not as "user-friendly" as those on, say, the Enterprise. Perhaps most notable are the automatic doors on DS9. These are large, round, cog-wheeled doors that roll noisily out of the way and then roll ominously shut. One gets the feeling that, while the smooth, almost soundless doors on board the Enterprise would not, and almost certainly could not, close on you, it seems likely that Cardassian safety features were not so rigorous, and that being caught in the way of one of these portals would really hurt.

In fact, this ties in with another underlying design concept. This is, after all, an alien space station, and it is doubtful whether any of the Federation personnel on board will ever be able to get used to living on DS9. Another factor contributing to this feeling is the imposing size of the sets for the show; looming bulkheads and support beams at odd angles everywhere, windows not quite shaped or set at the right level for humans and those damned doors just waiting to catch the heel of a slow-moving Ferengi.

To further enhance this off-balance sensation, Zimmerman designed a large viewscreen (larger than the one he created for the Enterprise of THE

NEXT GENERATION) that could be seen from both sides for DS9's operations center. This device is turned on only when needed. Gone is the Enterprise's familiar view of the stars, which always cuts back in when communications are terminated. On DS9, you actually see the viewscreen go off. A ring of blue neon (which necessitates shooting the effect with a green screen) gives a blurred edge to the viewscreen image, enhancing the alien look to its technology.

Another aspect of on-set effects that sets DEEP SPACE NINE apart from THE NEXT GENERATION is its use of real-time video monitors on the set with actual video images. This was made feasible by the development of techniques which can reduce video speed (a standard thirty frames-per-second) to the motion picture standard (twenty-four frames per second). With the image speeds matched in this fashion, it is now possible to film live video monitors without any image distortion. This is so effective that there are nearly seventy on-line video screens in use on the sets of DEEP SPACE NINE. The total cost?: nearly forty-five thousand dollars!

Another interesting detail can be found in the Holo-suites above the Promenade. Paramount's PR people insist (a bit too loudly, perhaps) that they are not being used for any sort of sexual activities. Unfortunately the actors state otherwise, particularly Armin Shimmerman. Plus the episode "Move Along Home" makes it very clear in the dialogue that this is exactly what the holo-suites are used for. Again, in keeping with the Cardassian design concept, they reveal the bulky holograph-producing machinery when they are shut off, as opposed to the clean yellow grid pattern seen when an Enterprise holodeck shuts down on THE NEXT GENERATION.

The opening title sequence of DEEP SPACE NINE was visually realized by special effects maven Dan Curry (whose NEXT GENERATION credits are lengthy). The sequence itself was designed and storyboarded by Richard Delgado, an illustrator whose bosses are Herman Zimmerman and Rick Sternbach. Pre-production illustrations are Delgado's specialty. Much of the look of DEEP SPACE NINE can be directly attributed to this talented artist, who came to the new series with no previous experience working on a Trek-related project.

Influenced largely by the work of French artist Jean Giraud (a.k.a. Moebius), Delgado designed many of the essential but unobtrusive background details of many of the show's sets in his meticulous designs. An interplanetary banking station and a Twenty-Fourth Century ATM was incorporated into the Promenade set and built directly from Delgado's designs. In fact, much of the Promenade was the creation of Delgado, from alien plants to shop designs. The only complaint Delgado seems to have about his job is that his boss, Herman Zimmerman, seems to find Delgado's sketches more effective when turned upside down.

Bunks in the former Cardassian quarters were also Delgado's design. Although not yet used on screen, Cardassian bunk beds come equipped with a force field, in case someone tries to assassinate the sleeper. This too was Delgado's idea.

The actual design of the space station exterior (the largest version being a six-foot model) was the work of many hands. Other hands beside those of Delgado contributed to its design, including those of Rick Sternbach, Mike Okuda, set designers Joe Hodges and Nathan Crowley, and scenic artists Denise Okuda and Doug Drexler.

FILMING DS9 : MARVIN RUSH

DEEP SPACE NINE's chief of photography is none other than Marvin Rush, who held that same position on THE NEXT GENERATION for three seasons. (Rush's job on THE NEXT GENERATION has been assumed by the talented cameraman Jonathan West.) In switching shows, Rush finds himself faced with a job of an entirely different scale.

What faces him is this fact: the sets for DEEP SPACE NINE are radically different from those for STAR TREK: THE NEXT GENERATION. They are much larger. New sets on recent NEXT GENERATION episodes have been things along the lines of Jeffrey Tubes intersections and the like. There are no new, large structures likely to turn up on the Enterprise (despite the many visually unexplored areas on board that immense ship). This is clearly not the state of things on DEEP SPACE NINE. Utilizing sets on three sound stages at Paramount Studios, including Sound Stages Four and Seventeen, DEEP SPACE NINE boasts two large, multiple-leveled sets: the Ops Center and Quark's Promenade. These sets are built more in the manner of feature film sets. Paramount has been more than willing to lavish large sums of money on the series they hope will be another smash syndication success for them.

These sets present a wide range of filming options. Camera moves on the large, sometimes complicated sets of DS9 are not so simple. This presents a much wider range of options in terms of camera movement and techniques than is generally permitted by THE NEXT GENERATION's format rules.

On one hand, DEEP SPACE NINE has much more room for crane shots than THE NEXT GENERATION ever allowed. (Luckily, Rick Berman is no Guy Caballero in this department.) On the other hand, the cameras on DEEP SPACE NINE may on many occasions be obliged to make a sudden transition from the wide-open spaces of the Promenade to the dim, cramped spaces of one of the many small shops which fill that space. While very large, the space station DS9 has many obscure corners. All in all, there are many challenges waiting for Marvin Rush and his DEEP SPACE NINE camera crew.

Like producers Rick Berman and Michael Piller, Emmy winning makeup artist Michael Westmore now has two full time jobs: THE NEXT GENERATION and DEEP SPACE NINE. Fortunately, he has an able staff of assistants to help him out on DS9: Craig Reardon, Jill Rockow and Janna Phillips. Janna Phillips is the daughter of Fred Phillips, the very first STAR TREK makeup artist. The man who designed the ears of Spock himself!

DEEP SPACE NINE calls for so many aliens that Westmore is no longer constrained by THE NEXT GENERATION's rule that new aliens must be designed for a specific script. On DEEP SPACE NINE, he can create aliens at will. Some will wind up as characters, and some will become an essential part of the background scenery.

One such character is the hulking Lurian, an alien who has been seen but not really included in any plotlines yet. This far he/it seems to be one of Quark's most reliable bar customers— sort of the Norm Petersen of the Twenty-Fourth Century. Some creatures created for DEEP SPACE NINE have also shown up in Ten Forward on THE NEXT GENERATION, raising the interesting question—are some of these creatures simply intergalactic bar hoppers out on a never ending binge?

Some aliens from THE NEXT GENERATION also show up on DEEP SPACE NINE. Viewers of the pilot episode, "Emissary," undoubtedly noticed that one of Benjamin Sisko's command officers during the battle with the Borg was a blue skinned Bolin, a race first encountered on THE NEXT GENERATION in the character of Captain Picard's talkative barber.

CREATION

The most prominent NEXT GENERATION alien crossover (after the Ferengi and the Cardassians) is the character of Jadzia Dax, who is a member of the Trill— a race first encountered in the NEXT GENERATION episode "The Host."

The Trill ambassador featured in that episode had a significantly different appearance than Dax does: it was more of a nose and forehead make-up effect which was dropped for the Trill character on DEEP SPACE NINE. For her portrayal of Jadzia Dax, Terry Farrell, fortunately, does not need to hide her attractive features behind any sort of appliance. In her case her "Trillness" derives from her spots, which start at her hairline and run down the side of her face, her neck and presumably beyond. In "Emissary," a glimpse is had of more of her spots, at least as far down as the top of her shoulders. Westmore applies the spotting himself on a daily basis.

As if to compensate for the change in Trill appearance, Westmore's facial appliance for Rene Auberjonois' shape-shifting character of Odo is quite an extensive prosthetic, one that effectively "runs" his facial features together.

And so, with a brilliant team at work, all the elements needed to get DEEP SPACE NINE on the air are in place: script, sets, special effects, actors and their make-up. A major investment for Paramount, and a labor of love for all involved, the new series looks great, and promises to be a worthy addition to the ongoing legacy of Gene Roddenberry's lasting creation.

STAR TREK premiered in 1966. Twenty-one years later the first STAR TREK spin-off, STAR TREK—THE NEXT GENERATION, hit the TV screen. The unprecedented seven year success of THE NEXT GENERATION led to DEEP SPACE NINE, the third STAR TREK series.

BEHIND THE SCENES

by W.D. Kilpack III and James Van Hise

STAR TREK—DEEP SPACE NINE will be the next giant in the one-hour syndicated drama category. The series, already the second most popular syndicated show, attracts over 15 million weekly watchers. Sister series STAR TREK—THE NEXT GENERATION runs first with 20 million regular viewers.

DEEP SPACE NINE presents darker, grittier stories than NEXT GENERATION. It offers more action and humor, like the original STAR TREK.

Tales told on DEEP SPACE NINE take place on a space station, a starfaring sailor's port of call. Aliens and situations never seen aboard a Federation starship often appear, including a Ferengi-run casino with a holographic brothel.

DEEP SPACE NINE shares incredible visual effects with NEXT GENERATION. Set in 2369, around the same time as NEXT GENERATION, some characters and locations appear on both series.

The alien space station, DEEP SPACE NINE, sits near the only known stable wormhole. The wormhole offers an interstellar passage beyond Federation space.

This provides the setting for the series. An equally interesting story lurks behind the scenes of the formerly Cardassian space station. Troubles in casting and design started at the very beginning.

According to the official legend, Berman and Piller worked on spin-off ideas for some time before refining DEEP SPACE NINE in October 1991. Because NEXT GENERATION still appeared in first run episodes, the new series had to be set in the same time frame. Otherwise complications would abound.

DEEP SPACE NINE was born into a universe ripe for exploitation. It could include the established conflict between Bajorans and Cardassians as the hub of the new series.

The Ferengi had faded into the background on STAR TREK—THE NEXT GENERATION. Their treatment on DEEP SPACE NINE is not ambitious but there is on-going development.

DARK TREK

Paramount announced plans for DEEP SPACE NINE in late 1991, shortly after the death of Gene Roddenberry. Early press reports proved inaccurate even when the news came from DEEP SPACE NINE co-creator Rick Berman.

Berman claimed the new series would be, "darker and grittier than THE NEXT GENERATION. The characters won't be squeaky clean." This disturbed long time Trek fans, but their fears proved groundless. While not as pristine as NEXT GENERATION, DS9 is no darker or grittier than the original STAR TREK.

Executive producer and co-creator Michael Piller said, "The vision of Gene Roddenberry was the inspiration for this series. [DEEP SPACE NINE is] optimistic and hopeful and constructive in how it approaches the future of humankind Gene designed for STAR TREK."

The optimistic future became clear in the second season episode "The Maquis." A scene shows Sisko telling Major Kira, "On Earth there is no poverty, no crime, no war." This is the first overt statement describing Earth as a "paradise." That is what Gene Roddenberry fervently hoped humanity would achieve by the 24th Century.

Rick Berman, the other creator and executive producer, said Roddenberry's universe provided an advantage from the start. He said, "It was a big gamble at first, and there have been other attempts [at science-fiction series] that have not paid off. The strength and familiarity of STAR TREK are not to be underrated. STAR TREK is not about the 24th Century. STAR TREK is about Roddenberry's vision of the 24th Century.

"I joined him knowing very little about STAR TREK and ended up carrying the flame for him. I learned Roddenberry's languages and beliefs. I became Roddenberry in absentia. Everything that STAR TREK has become is because of Roddenberry's influence on me."

Berman's fear of failed science fiction series was not misplaced. One example comes right from the Trekker camp. In 1977, STAR TREK II (not to be confused with the full-length feature film, STAR TREK II: THE WRATH OF KHAN) was proposed as a weekly series depicting a second five-year mission of the Enterprise under the command of Captain James T. Kirk, still played by William Shatner. Paramount would have syndicated the series. It was canceled two weeks before beginning principal photography.

Unlike with STAR TREK II, Paramount invested a stunning amount of money in DEEP SPACE NINE from the onset. Still, STAR TREK II's failure hung over the heads of the makers of DEEP SPACE NINE.

The third STAR TREK series was originally going to be called STAR TREK—THE FINAL FRONTIER. The space station floated on the frontier of space. Rick Berman and Michael Piller wanted the space station to have a Starbase number instead of a strange Bajoran or Cardassian name. This led to the final title.

Gene Roddenberry contributed little to the creation of DEEP SPACE NINE. Berman and Piller showed Roddenberry the concept a few months before his death. Differing reports say Roddenberry either approved of the idea or disliked it. No word of the spin-off leaked out until a few weeks after Roddenberry died.

The impetus for a new STAR TREK series came from Brandon Tarticoff, then head of Paramount. He told Rick Berman the studio wanted a second STAR TREK series to run concurrently with THE NEXT GENERATION. The proposal for DEEP SPACE NINE soon followed.

Tarticoff suggested that DEEP SPACE NINE be set on the frontier and contain elements of THE RIFLEMAN. Although Berman and Piller didn't follow that template, they adopted the idea of the main character being a widower raising his son.

PLANNING FOR THE FUTURE

In 1991 Paramount decided THE NEXT GENERATION would run seven seasons. This would give DEEP SPACE NINE crossover support for a year and a half after its January 1993 debut. At the time Paramount denied this plan but it is exactly what happened.

When development first began for DEEP SPACE NINE, the STAR TREK universe was already well defined. The Bajorans had been introduced in the NEXT GENERATION episode, "Ensign Ro," when Ro Laren (Michele Forbes) became a very popular character although not a regular cast member.

"Ensign Ro," and later, "The Wounded," told of the planet Bajor, a world conquered fifty years before by ruthless aliens known as the Cardassians. The Nazi-like Cardassians stripped the planet of natural resources using Bajorans as slave labor.

After forty years of Bajoran terrorism and the mining out of the planet, the Cardassians freed Bajor. The Bajorans immediately sought membership in the Federation, asking Starfleet to run the formerly Cardassian space station.

The first episode of DEEP SPACE NINE explores Bajoran culture and religion. The Kai Opaka appears in crucial scenes in "The Emissary." Not long after, in "Battle Lines," her character is written out of the series, leaving Bajor in religious turmoil.

The Kai serves a comparable role to the Pope in the Catholic Church, except the Kai can be male or female. The Kai Opaka is an almost beatific woman who practices what she preaches.

Kai Winn, a vengeful power-seeker succeeds her. Winn tries to assassinate her opponent.

DEEP SPACE NINE shows a Bajor stripped of mineral wealth by Bajorans enslaved in forced labor camps. Gallitepp was the most notorious camp (see "Duet").

The series explores Bajoran culture in "The Storyteller," "Cardassians" and "Sanctuary," continuing in season two with "Homecoming," "The Siege," "The Circle" and "The Collaborator." A provisional government now rules Bajor, but religion influences policy as Bajor appears to be a theocracy.

Alien worlds on STAR TREK usually have one world government. How this came about is never addressed.

Piller and Berman set DEEP SPACE NINE in the midst of Bajor and its conflict with the Cardassians. Piller, head of the script department of NEXT GENERATION, said, "One of the primary goals in making this series is to do something we didn't have the opportunity to do in NEXT GENERATION.

"Gene [Roddenberry] felt that the human being would evolve sufficiently by the 24th Century to lose the petty jealousies and the character flaws that hound us in the 20th. What that does from the dramatic standpoint is to make it very difficult to get conflict between human beings. So we [Piller and Berman] felt that it was very important to put our characters in a situation that would have inherent conflict."

Berman added, "DEEP SPACE NINE has more edge to it; we've got a remarkable cast of characters. We've got relationships that will accomplish what we couldn't on NEXT GENERATION. [The cast] is as good an ensemble as I've worked with."

A SPACE WESTERN

Michael Piller compares DEEP SPACE NINE to a Western with its fortress space station on the frontier of space. They almost called the show "THE FINAL FRONTIER." The frontier outpost hosts unusual visitors far from the well-traveled worlds of the Federation.

Rick Berman and Michael Piller considered setting the outpost on the surface of a planet as a cosmopolitan trading hub similar to Hong Kong. Exteriors would have been filmed at standing sets built north of Los Angeles in a desert area. Ultimately they decided that a space station located near a wormhole would be more visually interesting.

Building the massive exterior sets for the planetary setting would have been very expensive. The only exterior set used now is a miniature space station.

Setting the series on the surface of Bajor instead of in orbit would have changed storylines. Deep Space Nine no longer orbits Bajor since it was moved in the first episode.

They spent $12 million for the first two-hour introductory episode, including building the initial space station sets. Early script drafts featured a more run-down space station than finally portrayed.

Technology was to have lagged far behind that of the Federation. Yet the Cardassians had already been shown as more advanced than the Bajorans. They finally decided to make it modern but different from Federation stations.

Writing during the summer of 1992, shortly after the Los Angeles riots, inspired Michael Piller to have the Cardassians plunder the space station as they evacuated. They left the Federation a post with consoles stripped of vital components. They may have even carried off sofas, stereos and VCRs.

Herman Zimmerman designed the sets for DEEP SPACE NINE as he had for the last two STAR TREK films and the first season of THE NEXT GENERATION. The sets cost two million dollars, even more than the sets for an average STAR TREK motion picture. Sets for movies can be redressed from other films or TV series. DEEP SPACE NINE was brand new with a completely different look than what had come before.

Joe Hodges and Nathan Cowley supervised the construction of the sets based on Zimmerman's designs. Unlike the sets for Federation ships and stations, observation ports filled the office of the commander. Gul Dukat needed to see everything happening around him because of Bajoran terrorists during the occupation.

TECHNICAL CHALLENGES

The main corridor doors differ from anything previously seen on STAR TREK. They resemble those of a submarine more than a starship.

Zimmerman also conceived a viewscreen design visible from either side of the Operations Center. It dominates the Ops area but is activated only as needed.

The video monitors in Ops employ special images keyed to the speed of the motion picture camera. Video and film use different numbers of frames per second. Solving this technical problem created a smoother look for the monitor screens.

Richard Delgado storyboarded and designed the opening title sequence used for each episode. Special effects expert Dan Curry supervised the sequence.

Delgado also designed many of the background elements of DEEP SPACE NINE, including a 24th century ATM and some shops on the Promenade. Curry is a veteran of THE NEXT GENERATION.

Many people worked on the unusual, crab-like space station. Delgado, Herman Zimmerman, Mike Okuda, Denise Okuda, Rick Sternbach, Joe Hodges, Nathan Crowley and Doug Drexler designed various elements. The model for filming is approximately six feet long.

Michael Westmore and his staff create the aliens seen on DEEP SPACE NINE and THE NEXT GENERATION. Westmore often designs the aliens then executes the final look along with his staff. His staff included talented makeup technicians such as Craig Reardon (veteran of E.T. and POLTERGEIST), Janna Phillips (daughter of the late Fred Phillips, who worked on the original STAR TREK) and Jill Rockow.

Images from THE NEXT GENERATION helped in the design of the Cardassians, a sophisticated and powerful, militaristic race for whom beauty only exists together with strength.

Robert Blackman designed the Cardassian armor-like costumes, suggesting an exterior skeletal structure similar to crustaceans. Their grotesque facial structures were designed by Michael Westmore.

Cardassians are aggressive, quick to anger and abhor weakness. This, coupled with the of Berman and Piller's requirements, left little to work from. The instructions were concepts, not concrete designs. Three months before the scheduled date for set construction, the designers still stared at a blank page, far from the striking, spidery look of the final space station. After two more months, they began building.

During the two months DEEP SPACE NINE changed from looking like a North Sea oil rig to a thousand-year-old, rusted-out mining colony built by an unknown alien race to a series of diverse structural elements randomly pieced together over time with no apparent plan. Sketches, computer drawings and models were made for each option, then scrapped. Piller and Berman finally chose a futuristic, technologically advanced, alien structure.

The designers decided Cardassians liked things in orderly sets of three, the basis for the space-station design. DEEP SPACE NINE has three concentric rings as major structural components, plus three connector tunnels, or spokes, joining the major rings, three vertical docking pylons and three vertical weapons towers.

REDEFINING THE SPACE STATION

Zimmerman described the station, saying, "The Cardassian mind prefers balance to symmetry, ellipses to circles, angles to straight lines, and hard metallic surfaces and dark colors. They don't like ninety-degree angles. Cardassians believe in honesty in design and want to see the columns and beams that make up a structure rather than disguising them with some cosmetic treatment."

The jagged, abrupt hallways lack soft lighting and rounded contours. The dark Ops Center appears very alien, unlike anything else in the Trekker universe. It looks like a bunch of high-tech machinery stuck together with twine and chewing gum.

Designs for the interior of the station and the Promenade deck were still needed. Scenic artist assistant Doug Drexler, a previous recipient of an Oscar for his work in DICK TRACY, undertook the challenge of the Promenade. This gave the make-up crew more creative time.

Drexler said, "Roddenberry didn't want a STAR WARS feel to NEXT GENERATION. Still, even with this show, the aliens are us; the aliens are different slices of human beings. We should see ourselves in them."

The Promenade underwent a heavy facelift after the first season. "We wanted more bustle," Berman said. "[In the first season] we had all these well-dressed Bajoran women browsing around the station as if they beamed up for a little afternoon shopping.
"[We made] it look more like the part of town where sailors hang out; less like Beverly Center and more like a remote outpost in space."

Criticism hounded the first season. Critics bemoaned boring stories and shallow characters. Rumors predicted that Avery Brooks, who plays Commander Benjamin Sisko, would be dropped. The press charged that the Ferengi casino owner, Quark, played by Armin Shimmerman, was an anti-Semitic stereotype.

DEEP SPACE NINE co-producer and writer Peter Alan Fields said, "I don't think there's any less depth of character on the Enterprise [than on DEEP SPACE NINE]; it's just all been smoothed out. On DEEP SPACE NINE, they haven't been."

Shimmerman played two Ferengi characters for NEXT GENERATION. He said, "People are entitled to their opinions. Any time you're in the public eye, there's going to be gossip and stories. That doesn't mean I have to take it seriously."

He readily admits it is fun to play Quark, explaining, "All actors bring a part of themselves to their roles. Whatever part of me that is Quark has somehow risen to the top."

After the rest of the people working on DEEP SPACE NINE followed suit much of the criticism subsided. Brooks described the first season as being "like a first date with the show."

He continued, saying, "Now we're all in the throes of a full-fledged love affair." DEEP SPACE NINE still needs to establish direction, especially as the only Trek franchise airing new episodes for TV.

The creative team behind DEEP SPACE NINE worked very hard. They received only criticism for their first year's efforts. Much of the criticism resulted from high expectations arising because the creative team behind NEXT GENERATION formed the core of the crew for DEEP SPACE NINE.

Before the two-hour premier of DEEP SPACE NINE aired, Berman said that using the same production and postproduction group as NEXT GENERATION would make it easier to break in new crew members. He explained, "We've got a family here that's worked together for years and has done some wonderful stuff. It's like a rebirth."

BREAKING NEW GROUND

The experienced creative team and established storyline failed to give a strong start to DEEP SPACE NINE. Piller and Berman wanted to break new ground. That began with Commander. Benjamin Sisko.

Piller said, "We wanted to create a new kind of STAR TREK hero, a man who is not just the Starfleet officer who has given up family for career, like Picard; nor like Kirk, who's one of the boys on a great adventure. He is a man who has had a family and has lost a wife he loved and must raise a son."

Brooks said his "very human" character avoids the military strictures adorning many Starfleet officers. He said of his character, "So much of the military veneer is not there. He expresses what he feels. He isn't particularly interested in being here [DEEP SPACE NINE]. He's following orders. He's worried about raising his son in this environment. This station has been devastated."

Odo, portrayed by Rene Auberjonois, also breaks new ground. Auberjonois previously played Col. West in STAR TREK VI: THE UNDISCOVERED COUNTRY. Odo, the security officer, is roughly the counterpart of the original series' Spock or NEXT GENERATION's Data.

Odo is more complex than the others. He is a true mystery. Auberjonois says, "He's a shapeshifter. In the pilot, he says, 'I don't know where I came from; I don't know if there's anyone else like me; I've always had to pass myself off as human.' Odo was found floating in a star belt. Nobody knows what he is or where he came from."

This bears similarity to Data's origins, but Odo, a liquid plasma being, is not an emotionless android. He doesn't want to be human or Vulcan and still searches for identity.

Cirroc Lofton also breaks the mold with his portrayal of Sisko's 14-year-old son, Jake. Unlike NEXT GENERATION's Wesley Crusher, Jake has a father. Lofton believes his character gives DEEP SPACE NINE family appeal.

By the end of the second season, Cirroc had turned 16. While he still looks young, he is now as tall as Avery Brooks.

Siddig El Fadil portrays Dr. Julian Bashir as a fresh-from-Starfleet academy doctor who passed with flying colors. He chose DEEP SPACE NINE as his station because he specializes in alien life forms. El Fadil says his character is "confident because he's quite brilliant, but in real life, he's liable to make some mistakes because real life doesn't work as well as textbooks do."

Major Kira Nerys, the crucial character played by Nana Visitor, nearly missed the cut. Piller revealed, "We created the Ensign Ro character [for NEXT GENERATION] and a situation that was sort of a Palestinian- or Israeli- or American Indian-tale situation of disenfranchised people dominated for years. Unfortunately, the actress who plays Ro wasn't interested in a series. We had to write her out so that the situation remained. However, from this we established one of the most interesting relationships, which is that of Major Kira."

Visitor said Kira is a former Bajoran terrorist, "an absolute nationalist." This absolutist attitude gives her character a strong personality. Visitor observed, "Science fiction is really hard to do. You can put in all the fancy hardware you want, but if you don't get the people just right, you lose your audience's attention."

Paul Lynch directed the first one-hour episode of DEEP SPACE NINE. He said, "DEEP SPACE NINE is a little darker; there's a greater cross section of creatures and activity and conflict. It's still a family show, but it can deal with other things and has a greater scope than NEXT GENERATION. I think we're going to have stranger and weirder here [in DEEP SPACE NINE]. Even the main characters will take some odd turns."

Supervising Producer Ira Steven Behr added, "As characters, there's a certain lack of control they have over their lives."

THE LANGUAGE OF BELIEVABILITY

Creating the setting proved a challenge. Knowing DEEP SPACE NINE would orbit Bajor doesn't reveal how it will look and feel. That task fell to Rick Sternbach, graphic designer, and Herman Zimmerman, production designer.

Nothing could be "picked up" and used in the show. Everything had to be designed from scratch. As Berman put it, "You don't go to Bullock's to buy an outfit for a Ventaxian. You don't go into the scenery docks to pull out the bridge of a Cardassian warship. There are no books to tell you how to form a prosthetic to create a Ferengi head or how to build a model for a Pakled cargo vessel."

Berman believes drama relies on illusion. Few projects do so to as much as Star Trek. Every design comes from imagination.

Sternbach said, "Our goal is to do consistent science. DEEP SPACE NINE might have more action, more adventure. Still, there will be the same constraints, the same philosophy. We believe STAR TREK has the responsibility to society to teach something as well as entertain. Trek doesn't exist to beat people over the head with lessons. Yet when you total up all the episodes, you'll find many will be good lessons that won't be pedantic — not just for kids, but for everyone."

Graphic designer Michael Okuda added, "I'm proud of the fact that these [Trekker series] are the only shows on TV that say, 'Science is neat; science is fun; science is an endeavor worth pursuing.'"

Roddenberry hoped STAR TREK would show people the importance of science and space exploration. DEEP SPACE NINE achieves this goal.

Every astronomical event, including the Bajoran wormhole, is based on the latest scientific research supplied by companies including Apple Computer, Boeing Corp., Enterprise Institute, McDonnell Douglas, RAND Corp., UC-Irvine, Rockwell International, YPS, and yes, even NASA. Piller said, "We feel very strongly, in the spirit of Roddenberry, that the science should be credible. This is not a fantasy. If there is something weird and fantastic, then we must find a way to give it some basis in science as grounding."

NEXT GENERATION followed this course for years. DEEP SPACE NINE stepped into new waters with the space station.

Roddenberry once said, "The Starship Enterprise is not a collection of motion picture sets or a model used in visual effects. It is a very real vehicle; one designed for storytelling."

Piller and Berman wanted the same for their space station. The creative team made consistency their rule. Piller and Berman deemed the station a principal character in the series. The Enterprise played this role in the original series and NEXT GENERATION.

The producers wanted the station to be recognized at a glance, even at great distance. They also wanted it to exhibit bizarre alien architecture at close range.

Zimmerman raved about the miniature for the station, saying it was "incredible." He deemed the DEEP SPACE NINE model, "the best miniature I've ever seen."

Designing the space station proved to be the greatest challenge in creating the series. Several renditions were discarded along the road.

THE CHARACTERS

Originally Rick Berman described DEEP SPACE NINE as different from the STAR TREK universe. He said the crew on the Enterprise in NEXT GENERATION represented humanity at its ideal with few interpersonal conflicts, unlike the strong disagreements between Kirk, McCoy and Spock on the original STAR TREK. Berman wanted his new series characters to interact in dramatic ways with personal conflicts.

Commander Sisko initially had problems with Major Kira. This passed quickly as they grew to understand and respect each other. Sisko gets along with everyone on his staff now.

His only confrontation came in "Blood Oath" when he tried to forbid Jadzia Dax from fighting and killing. She said she would anyway and it would be up to him to allow her to resume her duties when she returned. Sisko said nothing more.

Former terrorist and Bajoran liaison to Deep Space Nine Major Kira Nerys finds Dr. Bashir hard to take. This is a minor personality clash. She gets along perfectly fine with everyone else except Quark, whom she truly despises. She dislikes all Ferengi due to their crude manners.

Major Kira real problem is Vedek Winn, who became Kai Winn in "The Collaborator." Kira believes Winn only seeks power.

Odo is irascible. He gets along well with the Operations officers. His conflicts are with Quark. They began before the Federation came to Deep Space Nine. As head of security, Odo knows Quark is behind illegal trading on the station.

Odo also has problems with the scientist who raised him. The man wanted to treat Odo like a laboratory specimen. When Odo set out on his own, his foster father became very resentful. They haven't settled their differences.

Dr. Julian Bashir gets along with everyone but sometimes rubs people the wrong way. When he revealed his knowledge of Bajoran music, he put his foot in his mouth. He referred to a composer as "the best of the lot" as if the musician wasn't particularly memorable. For a time he pursued Jadzia Dax.

Julian's friendship with O'Brien runs hot and cold. He had a breakthrough in the episode "The Armageddon Game."

Jadzia Dax is the latest incarnation of Dax. As Curzon Dax, he was a close friend of Ben Sisko years before. Ben tries to adjust to his old friend's new form as their relationship continues. Jadzia appears friendly but distant, not close to anyone else.

She asked Kira what killing feels like. Kira gave an honest answer but told Commander Sisko about Dax's plans with the three Klingons. Dax enjoys the company of Ferengi, finding them a very interesting people.

Miles O'Brien suffers character conflict. He argued with his wife after they transferred to the space station because she had no job other than being Molly's mother.

O'Brien competes with Dr. Bashir. It is more a racquetball rivalry than a personal one, and he seems to have overcome his need to best her.

Miles and Julian are an odd couple. Their character differences form the core of several stories.

Miles ran into trouble with the Bajorans when his wife taught scientific explanations of the wormhole contrary to the Bajoran religion. He dislikes Cardassians, so they single him out to be framed for selling weapons to the Maquis.

Nobody likes Quark. Everyone hates or tolerates him. Only Dax enjoys the company of Ferengi. She plays a card game with them called Tongo and often wins.

Kira didn't hide her dislike of Quark, yet Quark used his resources to find her when she was kidnapped. She owes him, and hasn't been as harsh since.

The alternate universe Kira executed Quark for helping Terrans escape from her domain. Odo suspects Quark whenever skullduggery is discovered on the station. O'Brien is indifferent to Quark, as is Dr. Bashir.

Commander Sisko tolerates Quark's complaints and demands. They engaged in spirited conversation when Quark accused Sisko of being prejudiced against Ferengi. Quark asked a series of probing questions the commander couldn't answer. This was the first time Quark and Sisko interrelated on more than a passing basis. It could lead to interesting future stories.

A ROSY FUTURE

Dramatic conflict on DEEP SPACE NINE keeps Roddenberry's rules. Conflicts arise from situations not character clashes.

Conflict comes from outside the space station. Bajoran factions distrust the Federation and Cardassians belatedly realize they left too soon.

DEEP SPACE NINE presents fewer space battles than NEXT GENERATION. The final second season episode, "The Jem 'Hedar," signals a possible increase in action for season three.

NEXT GENERATION aired for seven years. It personifies STAR TREK to many people, yet the original STAR TREK clearly followed a different approach. DEEP SPACE carves out its own direction.

Nana Visitor may have said it best when she observed that since the first season, "We're getting it right." Zimmerman added, "If history is allowed to repeat itself, and if, as Gene Roddenberry once said, 'You can come home again,' then the world we have created for DEEP SPACE NINE will please the public, ring true — and, I hope, live long and prosper."

If ratings are any indication, Zimmerman has nothing to worry about.

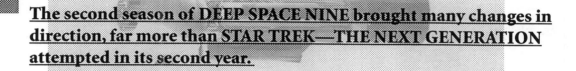

The second season of DEEP SPACE NINE brought many changes in direction, far more than STAR TREK—THE NEXT GENERATION attempted in its second year.

SEASON TWO: DEEP SPACE NINE

The second season of STAR TREK: DEEP SPACE NINE demonstrates new directions. It introduces new characters and expands the backgrounds of existing characters.

Season one established the premise. Space station Deep Space Nine orbited the Bajoran wormhole, a gateway through space connecting the Alpha Quadrant (Federation space) with the Gamma Quadrant hundreds of light years away.

The Gamma Quadrant contained many previously unknown worlds and races, although they are all conveniently humanoid with the same passions and drives as human beings. They look somewhat alien but don't act alien.

The only truly non-Terrestrial beings encountered in nearly 30 years of STAR TREK were in the NEXT GENERATION episode "Darmok." It was difficult to understand their alien thought processes.

What distinguishes DEEP SPACE NINE from previous STAR TREK is the narrowly defined region of space, bordered on one end by Bajor and on the other by the wormhole. While some episodes pass through the wormhole, they don't go very far. Federation penetration of Gamma Quadrant is not clearly defined.

Season two opened with a three part storyline consisting of "The Homecoming," "The Circle" and "The Siege." Political factions on Bajor demonstrate hostility towards the Federation. A new faction, The Circle, pushes for expulsion of the Federation from Bajor. This would leave the planet defenseless.

Richard Beymer plays Li Nalas, the hero of the Bajoran resistance rescued by Major Kira from a secret Cardassian prison camp. Li Nalas would have made an excellent addition to the cast of recurring characters.

Li Nalas demonstrated great internal conflict. His heroism arose from sheer luck when he surprised and killed a famed Cardassian military officer. Struggling Bajoran freedom fighters seized on the incident and made Li Nalas a symbol as if he had single-handedly destroyed a Cardassian battalion.

Although he understood that the Bajorans needed heroes in hard times, he felt guilty accepting honors he wasn't due. When he returned to Bajor, he wanted to live a normal life.

Instead he found himself manipulated by Bajoran factions. He could have emerged as a character learning to use his influence for good. Killing him was pointless.

BACK FROM THE PAST

Episodes such as "Invasive Procedures" spotlight less developed cast members, including Dax. Unfortunately, too often they only mark time, adding little to the series. In this episode, a rejected Trill candidate forces Jadzia's symbiont to be transplanted into him at gun point.

Actress Terry Farrell, who plays Dax, recently expressed interest in appearing on the Howard Stern radio show in New York. Stern said that since he considers her to be a "nobody," he wouldn't have her on unless she took off her blouse in the studio — not an unusual request for that show.

She declined. A lot more people watch DEEP SPACE NINE than listen to Howard Stern or watch his TV show.

The question of Cardassian war orphans is raised in an interesting episode, "Cardassians," involving the character Garak, played by Andrew Robinson. Robinson portrayed the serial killer in the original DIRTY HARRY movie two decades ago.

Gul Dukat also returns, as reprehensible as ever. Dukat is so reprehensible in "Cardassians" he separates a child from his father for several years as a political ploy. Cardassia's dirty politics appear in the episode, "Tribunal."

The title character of "Melora" comes from a low gravity world and uses leg braces and a wheelchair in Earth gravity. She was developed as a possible regular on the series;

The episode revealed much about Dax. It remains the best Dr. Bashir story to date.

Dax is underused on the series. The next episode revealed Quark becoming the most overused regular.

"Rules of Acquisition" is a Quark episode. It reveals a lot about the Ferengi, and shows the first Ferengi female. Ferengi women are supposed to stay at home and refrain from wearing clothes, a facet originally established in the first season of THE NEXT GENERATION. This liberated Ferengi female disguises herself as a man.

The scene in which the gender bender comes on to Quark, who doesn't know that Pel is a woman, is interesting. He seems to be responding even though he thinks that Pel is a man. The significance of that is quickly ignored.

This episode also features the return of the marvelously repulsive Grand Nagus, played by Wallace Shawn. This is a good Ferengi episode that balances story and characterization, unlike the later episode, "Profit And Loss," that tells two conflicting stories. In that one, Quark's tale comes across as completely unnecessary, and unbelievable.

"Necessary Evil" is a second season highlight which demonstrates why many episodes of DEEP SPACE NINE seem so tame and restrained. Ostensibly the story of how Odo became security chief under the Cardassians, the flashbacks to life on the space station under Gul Dukat show a very different atmosphere of darkness and dread. There is an alien ambiance missing from the pristine Federation-controlled Deep Space Nine. This episode is effective *film noir*.

Whenever this episode switches into the flashback mode, there is an air of repression as Odo moves down bustling, overcrowded corridors in search of the answer to a mystery. The one mystery never explained in that episode is why Odo kept his job when he failed to solve the crime he was appointed to investigate. Cardassians aren't forgiving.

"Second Sight" is a better than average Sisko episode in which his dream date turns out to be just that. The highlight of the episode is the performance of actor Richard Kiley as a brilliant scientist who wants to end his career on a high note. This episode gives Sisko more character scenes than any story since "Emissary," the premiere.

All too often Sisko comes across as narrow and restrained. Gul Dukat makes a joke about this at Sisko's expense in "The Maquis," so clearly the writers are aware of how underwritten his scenes tend to be in most episodes. Only occasionally are there interesting flashes of character, such as in such episodes as "The Collaborator," "Crossover" and "The Jem 'Hedar."

LIFE ABOARD A SPACE STATION

"Sanctuary" is better than most episodes of DEEP SPACE NINE. It shows what this series is capable of accomplishing when it isn't telling routine little space dramas. While the average episode of DEEP SPACE NINE isn't bad, neither is it very compelling.

Few series feature characters who babble as much as this one's do. It often tells rather than shows.

Sometimes what they babble about is worth hearing, such as when the space station finds itself besieged by three million refugees from the Gamma Quadrant. The woman who is appointed the spokesperson for the refugees emerges as an interesting character. The story deals with the very real problems faced when a society is confronted with a sudden massive influx of people from another culture.

This is a good Major Kira episode. The best DEEP SPACE NINE episodes draw parallels with our own reality such as in the first season show "Duet.". These outings are more rare than they should be.

"Rivals" is one of those marking time episodes which fills the hour without accomplishing a great deal. Dr. Bashir and Miles O'Brien have major character scenes. They make an interesting odd couple. Would that they were given something more interesting to do than play racquetball.

This story, while set in the future, ignores the fact that it's the future . The con artist in the story would be exposed in a moment due to information access in the 24th Century. He wouldn't have been conned by a woman selling him the equivalent of swamp land in Florida. He would have got on the 24th Century equivalent of the Net and downloaded the truth in no time. You can't set stories in the future unless you treat it as if it's the future.

"The Alternate" is another rare exploration of the life of Odo. It presents the Bajoran scientist who raised him and taught him to be humanoid. The scientist resented it when Odo chose to go off on his own.

It's the only "monster on the loose" episode of DEEP SPACE NINE to date. The episode is interesting for a number of reasons. They go to a planet in the Gamma Quadrant and find ancient artifacts that they bring back to the space station. The artifacts are a red herring. Something starts prowling around the space station at night. It seems the artifacts have something to do with it but it turns out that Odo has turned into his own evil twin.

CHARACTER SPOTLIGHTS

"Armageddon Game" makes no sense. A society is destroying a biological warfare agent which once decimated its populace and wants to kill anyone who knows how to make it. A cure for the agent now exists which ends any threat it could pose! The jeopardy seems artificial and the alien society a race of nitwits.

"Whispers" is DEEP SPACE NINE as if it were written by Philip K. Dick. It turns sense of reality on its head and keeps the viewer guessing right up to the end. It seems that key personnel on the space station were replaced by doubles. Actually something even more unusual is going on, and nobody is dreaming.

"Shadowplay" raises questions about technology and the nature of reality. It takes place on a planet in the Gamma Quadrant. It's another mystery with an ingenious solution. It raises the same questions as such THE NEXT GENERATION episodes as "The Big Goodbye" and "Elementary Dear Data." They still don't answer them. It's an interesting story just the same.

"Playing God" is a Dax episode. The story tries hard to give her dimension, but doesn't succeed. The only aspect of Jadzia Dax that has been interesting thus far is that she likes Ferengi. The producers knew this plot angle was weak and propped it up with a second story about a miniature universe threatening our own.

"Profit And Loss" is a Quark-in-love episode. It doesn't gel. It even uses the "woman from his past" cliché.

Quark comes across as overcooked or under developed depending on the storyline. He's consorted with murderers and delivered vital information crucial to saving Major Kira's life. He's been greedy and compassionate, untrustworthy and noble. It has never sorted itself out.

This episode is significant. It introduces a Cardassian anti-military underground. The Cardassian government shown in "Tribunal" clearly needs destabilizing.

"Blood Oath" is one of the five best episodes of DEEP SPACE NINE . It is the first to feature Klingons, not counting the walk-ons of the chef in "Melora" and "Playing God."

Three Klingons, Kang, Kor, and Koloth arrive on the space station looking for Dax. All three originally appeared in episodes of the original STAR TREK of the 1960s. They are played still played by the same three actors: Michael Ansara, John Colicos, and William Campbell. The story is structured just like Classic Trek. Everything leads up to a violent hand-to-hand combat scene in the climax. The story demonstrates why Klingons are much more interesting characters than their Federation counterparts.

If they really do another STAR TREK spin-off, it should be peopled with Klingons. Then we would see some real drama, conflict and action. Klingons don't do anything on a small scale.

"The Maquis" is padded to two-hours. It introduces a Federation underground resistance group fighting Cardassians in the demilitarized zone. Each side seems equally at fault . This storyline is a set-up for the much better NEXT GENERATION episode "Preemptive Strike" in which the Maquis are glorified and the Cardassians vilified.

"Crossover" is the unexpected sequel to the original STAR TREK episode "Mirror, Mirror." Major Kira and Dr. Bashir encounter a parallel universe. The alternate universe lacks the color and drama of the Jerome Bixby original.

The Empire of a century ago has been overthrown along with the colorful costumes. The episode shows very different versions of familiar characters, including Sisko. His duplicate is a pirate and stud horse for Intendent Kira. The normal Ben Sisko looks dull by comparison. It's fun to see a sequel to one of the all time favorite original STAR TREK episodes and hear them talk about Kirk and Spock.

THE FUTURE OF DEEP SPACE NINE

"The Collaborator" appeared to be a turning point effecting many storylines to come. The political and religious hierarchy on Bajor has a dramatic impact on Deep Space Nine. The

story also features the return of Louise Fletcher as Vedek Winn, last seen in the trilogy begun in season two.

The Maquis, introduced in "The Maquis," and the Dominion, introduced in "The Jem 'Hedar," will have a greater impact on the third season of DEEP SPACE NINE than will Winn . She may dislike the Federation, but, facing threats from the Maquis, the Cardassians, and the Dominion, she needs all the friends she can get.

"Tribunal" is an O'Brien episode. He is put on trial on the Cardassian homeworld. It is a science fiction version of Kafka's "The Trial." It works.

It also ties into the Maquis. It shows how desperate Cardassia is about the Maquis. They may be close to war. O'Brien now hates the Cardassians.

The season finale, "The Jem 'Hedar," is an unexpected wild card. It changes everything and will effect every storyline to come. The Dominion, a mysterious race referred to in passing in the episodes "Rules of Acquisition" and "Sanctuary," emerge from the shadows with frightening force.

Their military arm, the Jem 'Hedar, have closed the wormhole and forbidden Federation vessels from entering the Gamma Quadrant. They don't want to negotiate. They imprison Sisko and Quark and attack the starship Odyssey, an Enterprise lookalike. The Jem 'Hedar become a bigger menace than the Cardassians and the Romulans combined.

This is not a cliffhanger. The story is resolved. The menace of The Dominion will not be concluded in the third season premiere. Instead the Dominion will become to DEEP SPACE NINE what the old style Klingons were to STAR TREK in the 1960s. They are an on-going menace adding violent action to DEEP SPACE NINE .

The Dominion will also be an on-going threat on STAR TREK: VOYAGER set to premiere in 1995. THE NEXT GENERATION introduced the Cardassians in advance of the premiere of DEEP SPACE NINE. Now DEEP SPACE NINE does the same favor for VOYAGER.

STAR TREK has always had larger than life villains. In "The Jem' Hedar," one Dominion soldier says he looks forward to when he can meet a Klingon in combat. Many viewers would like to see this as well.

There have been questions about the future of DEEP SPACE NINE. Some say it's ratings aren't good. That isn't true. DS9 consistently rates in the top 10 syndicated TV shows. While TNG has ranked #1 or #2, DS9 reached as high as #4 and seldom fell lower than #7. In reruns in June 1994, THE NEXT GENERATION fell to fourth place and tied with DEEP SPACE NINE, which didn't lose any momentum.

Other syndicated science fiction TV series such as ROBOCOP, HIGHLANDER, BABYLON 5, TIME TRAX, and TEKWAR seldom, if ever, rise as high as #20. Whether DEEP SPACE NINE will rise to the solid #2 spot vacated by NEXT GENERATION will be determined in the 1994-95 television season. Its future is not in doubt, but only time will tell if it runs a full seven years.

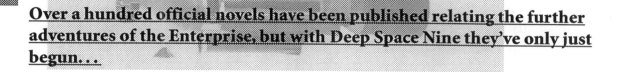

DEEP SPACE NINE BOOK REVIEWS

by Alex Burleson

BOOK #1: EMISSARY

J.M. Dillard

based on teleplay by Michael Piller of a story by Piller and Rick Berman.

Dillard's novel delves further into the psyche of Benjamin Sisko than the televised version, deepening Sisko's backstory and helping to explain his motivations. The demons confronting Ben shape his character — from the beginning of the novel to the way he finally expurgates the malignant guilt that has blinded him since his wife died in the Borg attack.

In the novel, we see how the attack at Wolf 359 changed the young first officer on his way up into an embittered victim who was ready to quit Starfleet, and life. Only the need of his son Jake kept him alive.

Kira did not believe the Federation had any business taking control of the abandoned Cardassian mining station in Bajoran space, now re christened Deep Space Nine by Starfleet. Sisko surprises her, as she found a begrudging respect for her new commander.

Kira is awed that he is called to Kai Opaka on Bajor, given an orb and then proclaimed "The Emissary," as foretold by the Bajoran prophets. He also gains her respect as he pitches in to clean up, getting his hands dirty alongside her, and plea bargaining with Quark to make the Ferengi do what he wants him to do.

Ben's treatment of Quark wins Odo's respect. The shape shifter did not think he would like the human commander, but anyone who can pull one over on Quark is worth considering.

We learn how Dax relived the joining ceremony, first as the symbiotic being removed from the dying Curzon Dax, then as the unjoined Jadzia, awaiting her destiny. We share the way the two beings merge as one, getting inside the Trill mindset.

The Cardassian bluster is great, but Kira's defiant stand on pride and principle resonates. We see just how important honor is to the young Bajoran.

Miles Edward O'Brien is great as he is forced to teach the computer how to act like one — despite the Cardassian personality it must overcome. It did not know how to bypass a safety system, yet O'Brien's fussing with his finicky nemesis rings true. O'Brien retains his "miracle worker" status; saving Odo by giving the Cardassian transporter a solid kick; finding Kira some shields after the classic "Shields up!," "What shields?" exchange; then masking the station so that the Cardassians would not be able to confirm that Kira was bluffing.

Bashir's character gets off to a slow start. We do begin to see just why the idealistic young surgeon is drawn by the adventure on Deep Space Nine assures.

We also see how Quark is planning to twist the new humans around his finger — and how surprised he is when Sisko turns the tables on him and uses Nog to force Quark's hand. Quark is forced to a wary respect for the new commander sharp enough to outwit the Ferengi entrepreneur at his own game.

BOOK #2: THE SIEGE
Peter David

This is another textbook Peter David novel in that the twists and turns run the gambit from comic to tragic, and the reader is never sure what to expect. Then comes a hard, fast gut punch of print about as subtle as an armed hand grenade.

Most writers of so-called 'comic-dramas' water down the story producing either a sitcom that's not funny or a drama ruined by humor at inappropriate moments. David separates the two elements, linking them into a completely interconnected storyline.

Peter's novels always mix the happy and kind with the sad and malevolent. He shows no sign of changing the style. This book is complex to extremes.

A Borg ship arrives through the wormhole, forcing Sisko and his son to relive the nightmare of Wolf 359. The ship is a red herring, arriving in pieces and establishing the anomaly that requires closing the wormhole.

Miles annoys Keiko and Odo with his attempt to learn slight-of-hand tricks to entertain Molly at her birthday party. Odo makes use of Miles' attempts as they help him formulate a plan to go after the serial killer. The novel has many subplots that weave together in the tapestry of the story making the whole greater than the sum of its parts.

A shape-shifting assassin arrives on Deep Space Nine and sets to work at his grim task. He taunts Odo and Sisko, leaving Arabic numbers to denote each slaying that takes place under their noses. His punishment seems to fit his crimes.

A vital sub-plot involves Dr. Bashir, forced to face a no-win 'Kobayashi Maru' type of medical ethics challenge. A group of religious zealots arrive at the station, en route to preach their religion in the Gamma Quadrant. Sisko notes a boy's poor demeanor and recommends a subterfuge to allow a medical examination.

The child of the high priest suffers from a fatal debilitating disease that is easily correctable, but the priest considers it divine judgment, forbidding treatment. Sisko considers it an open-and-shut Prime Directive case and forbids Julian to pursue the matter. Bashir is torn by repulsive options.

Bashir uses a holosuite recreation of what her son will look like as he dies to force the bereaved and bewildered mother to save her son. The cost will be her marriage and her heritage.

Mother and son are exiled forever. Peter makes us feel sad for the high priest as he explains that he must now live out his life without the love of his wife and son.

Bashir has so raked himself over the coals that we can only wonder what Sisko could do that would be worse. David leaves the question open-ended so our imagination must fill in the blanks, ending the story as Sisko calls the doctor.

Bashir secured the holosuite by blackmailing Quark into assisting him. He saved Quark's life from the shape-shifting assassin, but that was only good for free drinks. Bashir's ace was the holosuite program he caught Quark and a Ferengi rival enjoying. The two participated in a triple-X program complete with nude representations of Kira Nerys and Jadzia Dax.

Quark is horrified by what the two female officers, especially Kira, would do if they found out. Bashir makes Quark delete the offensive program.

This incident is later referred to in the DS9 novel FALLEN HEROES when Bashir tells Odo that Kira and Dax would appreciate his close monitoring of Quark's holosuite activity even if they don't know why.

Odo's payoff to O'Brien is classic, as is the juxtaposition of plot elements. The brutal serial killings prove a point and are not there just for the sensation. The killings are not gratuitous. Each plays an integral part in the story, but they are gruesome to read.

A religious fanatic is savagely bashed to death; a Bajoran mother and her child are terrorized, first by a Cardassian rapist, then by the assassin. The mother panics when Odo helps since she just saw the assassin assume the same form.

A beloved Bajoran dock master is the next victim. A nurse who works with Julian rounds out the random murders.

Each killing ups the ante one more chip. The first happens in seclusion to an unknown visitor. The aborted attack identifies the assassin as a shape shifter. The third attack occurs in a public area, forcing Sisko to inform the populace of the threat. Bashir interrupts an attempt on Quark and his Ferengi rival and lets Odo test himself against this fellow changeling.

Jake almost becomes victim four, forcing Ben to prove his Starfleet Academy nickname, "dead-eye," by banking a phaser shot off a mirror. Odo becomes a mirror forcing Ben to back up his boast with his son's life on the line.

Sharp comedy intertwines with tragedy as Julian throws out a gag password—"Kiss me, you fool!"—only to have it backfire. He finds that the assassin overheard the gag and wrote the password in blood over his friend's bludgeoned body.

Keiko and Molly are endangered as the assassin flees Odo into their quarters. Keiko gives Odo an edge at just the right moment. The passwords are inventive.

Then it's Odo pitted against his antagonist in a battle of wits. If one becomes a stone, the other becomes a drill. If one tries to drive a spike into the other's head, the other moves the head to another part of his body. This goes on and on.

Two security guards, among Worf's favorites in Peter's TNG novels STRIKE ZONE and A ROCK AND A HARD PLACE, are forced to face a practical joke by Nog. It could prove deadly. The officers comment on the surreal battle between the two implacable juggernauts.

The battle continues into space. Cardassian Gul Dukat comments on Odo's tenacity as he continues the changeling version of a Texas death-match.

In his opening remarks, David alludes that his research into Odo's ability to transform was extensive. He explains that showing Odo doing any of this in a DS9 episode would cost an entire season's budget to film.

This remarkable novel asks as many questions as it answers. It involves the reader in every facet of the story.

BOOK #3: BLOODLETTING

K.W. Jeter

Dr. Bashir stands up to Ben Sisko. The commander wants to send his medical quarantine section to the other end of the wormhole as a counter-weight to a Cardassian attempt to gain control of the Gamma Quadrant.

Kira adds a Bajoran presence and battles a former comrade who considers her a sellout. Julian meets the wormhole entities who take Kira's form to communicate with him.

Julian travels to the end of time to find an escape from the wormhole. His sensitivity to engines precludes travel by ships. That slows the story. O'Brien's interaction with Julian and intervention with the Cardassians lets O'Brien steal the show.

Odo arrests O'Brien and takes him to Ben after the chief tries to use a 'hammer' to put a round Federation 'peg' into a square Cardassian hole. Odo handcuffs O'Brien, but the Cardassians make a mistake. They use military arithmetic which Odo recognizes from the Cardassian occupation. This tips off Sisko and the others as to their intentions.

The story starts well. It loses force once Kira and Julian enter the wormhole. Julian's interaction with the 'prophets' is handled very differently than Sisko's encounter in the superior THE EMISSARY. They now understand linear time, using non-linear methods to transport Julian rather than undergoing head-death. The ride is harrowing, but Julian uses this four eon window in an incomprehensible astrophysical paradox that never gets off the ground.

BOOK #4: THE BIG GAME

Sandy Schofield

(with Dean Wesley Smith and Kristine Kathryn Rusch.)

Commander Riker sends his regrets to Quark before the championship poker game. That doesn't keep several other disparate characters from showing up. One rather obvious assassin comes to play, forcing Odo to learn the game as a ringer for Quark.

Time traveler and con man Berlinghoff Rassmussen, from the TNG episode "A Matter Of Time," shows up. So does Lursa and B'Etor of the Duras family in TNG episode "Redemption I/II" and DS9 episode "Past Prologue." Etaan, the woman who seduced Will Riker, then infiltrated the Enterprise with a mind control device in TNG episode "The Game," also joins the game.

Klingons, Romulans, Cardassians, Terrans and Ferengi join in the quest to be named top poker player in the quadrant. The winner pulls the ultimate double-cross on the double-crosser. Quark is forced to donate the pot to charity.

Julian's attempt to get into the game is interesting. The good doctor takes some of his own medicine as a flirtatious woman when a tribble starts to take the fun out of the party.

Lursa and B'Etor are up to no good, conspiring to fix the game. They try to entice Garak to join their club, but the Cardassian tailor shows his deep sense of honor and abstains. Garak is a student of poker and does not want to win by unfair advantage.

Garak's skills take him far, but he and everyone else must deal with Quark's attempt to fix the game. The Grand Nagus pulls his own scam on Quark, but Jake and Nog find out what they are up to.

The energy beings who live in another 'phase' are interesting. Kira tries to stop the senseless slaughter of the defenseless, gentle beings but inadvertently causes one's death. Sisko tries to console her, but she seems heartbroken by her act. Unlike Ben and Kira, the reader learns that the being is reborn as a multiple number of energy creatures.

Kira and Sisko, with Miles' help, overcome the pirates after a revelation by the assassin. Sisko agrees to free the killer much to Odo's chagrin. Ben wins back Odo's respect by lying to the assassin after he gets enough information to save the station.

The scenes at Ops are tense. Sisko, Kira, Dax and O'Brien attempt to compensate for the disruption in the natural flow of the space-time continuum. The senior staff deals with the assassin and the poaching pirates and ships from Bajor and Cardassia Prime blaming each other for starting the event sequence in motion. The Bajoran is as brusque as the Cardassian, putting even Kira to the test.

Sisko deals with stubborn Cardassians in classic form. His phase-jumps disable their spacecraft, a personal demonstration of what he has been saying all along.

The plot takes a back seat to the poker game, but the two meld to create a textured novel. The assassin and discovery of the pirates' true identity could have been more direct. It seems unlikely the pirate would drop by with the one obscure piece of information needed to solve the puzzle.

It seems unlikely Sisko would even consider information from such a source without proof. True, he is desperate, but why would the pirate enter the game and kill the other players if he knew what was really going on?

The 'big game' is first rate. Not quite a straight flush, but a solid full house.

BOOK #5: FALLEN HEROES
Dafydd ab Hugh

This is an extraordinary novel. The Deep Space Nine characters undergo brutal, painful deaths. The novel follows time travel, alternate universe conventions, much like the classic Trek novel THE ENTROPY EFFECT and the TNG episodes "Yesterday's Enterprise," "Parallels" and "All Good Things" as well as the TNG novel IMZADI, and the entire crew in "Yesterday's Enterprise" and "Cause And Effect."

Never before have so many main characters died such graphic, disturbing deaths. ab Hugh suggested his own tag line for this breathtaking novel: "Everybody dies!" That is not entirely accurate, but with four key exceptions it will suffice.

The highly structured book sends each hero to their death on their feet, each showing honor and courage worthy of a Klingon d'Har Master. It is the same story in each case, yet each is unique in the way the author invades the mind of each hero as they sacrifice their life.

Every heroic act weaves a multi-layered tapestry allowing the tragedy witnessed to be prevented only if Quark and Odo work together. The two shell shocked survivors add an eerie dimension to the story.

Miles O'Brien is maimed by a grenade and dies in agony using his last breath to claw his surroundings. Kira loses a leg yet refuses to surrender and is crushed by the very runabout she risked her life to launch. Morbid yet mesmerizing.

Odo and Quark gather information as to what happened at the decaying station. They find each body of a loved one and the story flashes back to how each died in this alternate universe.

Keiko is found dead in her classroom using her final seconds to save Molly, Jake and Nog. O'Brien outlives Keiko but loses the spark of life and is almost blessed by his grisly death.

The first two discoveries deliver a backstory. As O'Brien transports in seconds too late, he sees his beloved shot in the head with an armored projectile.

His attempt at suicide fails when an invader shields him from the blast of his kamikaze phaser grenade. O'Brien then arms the attack teams he leads with outclassed weapons.

Miles is taken by a Bajoran militia leader, a feisty older version of Kira. O'Brien forgets to set the timer on his phaser grenade and is slowly killed as half of his body is destroyed.

Odo and Quark are numbed by shock. They begin to piece the bloody jigsaw puzzle together.

The next valiant warriors to die are Jadzia, Dax and Kira Nerys. Jadzia is killed by the initial bullet to the head. Dax, the symbiotic, outlives the host and gains revenge for both by killing the invader whose body did not vanish.

Host and symbiotic are unable to replicate Klingon firearms, but quick post mortal reflexes give Odo and Quark a key piece of the puzzle. Each death furthers Odo and Quark toward the solution.

Kira takes out an entire company of invaders. After she disarms one she turns the weapon against the attackers. She is injured in battle but still launches the runabout full of children. Bitter The same ship crushes her. When alien phasers damage the ship, the panicked pilot takes out the entire runabout deck.

Odo is deeply moved by his friend's passing. So, surprisingly, is Quark. When they notice an attempt to honor a body, the two time-travelers realize someone is still alive.

The next cadaver belongs to Julian. He entered vital information into his medical log, allowing Odo and Quark to finally understand what has happened. They meet two traumatized children, the only survivors of the holocaust.

Odo forces Jake to tell them what happened to Nog and Sisko. Jake, and 'his' child, Molly Worf O'Brien, survived Sisko's ingenious method of wiping out the threat. An especially touching moment occurs when the Jake of that future sacrifices his and Molly's existence to allow Odo and Quark to fix the space time continuum.

Odo becomes liquefied by their plan, forcing a half-naked Quark to run into Ops with vital information. The future rests on Sisko and Kira agreeing to trust the 24th Century "Scrooge." Only he knows what Christmas-yet-to-come will look like.

BOOK #6: BETRAYAL

Lois Tilton

A sympathetic Cardassian stowaway slips on board DS9. Nog locates the stowaway and blackmails him into fixing things around the station.

Nog is found out by Quark, who takes over. Then Jake shows honor by keeping Nog's secret although Sisko questions his judgment.

O'Brien is impressed and offers the stowaway a job. Sisko wants to turn the prisoner over to an angry Cardassian captain. Jake then barges in and tells of the woes suffered by the defector. He had been forced to watch as his father and brothers were hanged over a several day period.

Sisko and O'Brien turn the Cardassians' plot against them, warning the captain what he is about to do. Predictably, the captain thinks it a trick.

An interesting subplot involves a monk important to Kira. It is the "Betrayal" referred to by the title. His unclear motivations prove less noble than Kai Opaka's betrayal in the DEEP SPACE NINE episode, "The Collaborator."

The Kai gave her own son to prevent a great slaughter. The monk wants money and lacks concern for his people's plight under Cardassian rule. Not even a Ferengi would sell out his race for a handful of gold-pressed latinum.

It causes Kira to further doubt her faith. The doubts will increase in the DEEP SPACE NINE episode "The Collaborator."

The relationship between the defector and Jake allows Sisko to see that his son is maturing. His information proves vital. The betrayer soon finds his rank of Glen riding on the fate of Gul Dukat. Sisko and Kira find they miss the familiar evil of Dukat when confronted with this new, unstable evil that threatens Bajor and Cardassia Prime.

The story shows the similarity of Cardassians and Bajorans, while accenting the differences. A good Cardassian helps Terrans and Bajorans against bad Cardassians while a bad Bajoran helps the bad Cardassians. The juxtaposition of roles is striking. Subtle character shadings bring home the message.

These are the only DEEP SPACE NINE novels published at this time. There have only been half a dozen. As DEEP SPACE NINE rolls on, the tie-in books will continue and their new adventures will be chronicled.

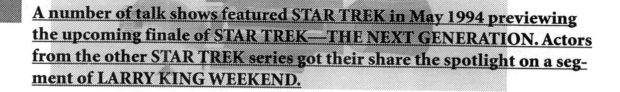
THE CAST OF DS9 ON LARRY KING LIVE

The impending end of first run episodes of NEXT GENERATION attracted media attention. Actors from the series appeared on national talk shows. On May 14, 1994, LARRY KING WEEKEND featured cast from both STAR TREK—THE NEXT GENERATION and DEEP SPACE NINE.

The guest line-up included Marina Sirtis, Michael Dorn, Avery Brooks, Nana Visitor, Rene Auberjonois and writer/producer Rick Berman.

Larry King had trouble with Rene's name, mispronouncing it as "Rene Aubujolais."

Rick Berman led off as executive producer of DEEP SPACE NINE, THE NEXT GENERATION and STAR TREK: VOYAGER. He said he first became involved with STAR TREK in the early 1980s while working at Paramount Pictures as a studio executive.

Paramount assigned Berman, then the lowest tenured vice-president, to work with Gene Roddenberry. No one else wanted the job because Roddenberry had a reputation for being difficult.

"In the very first meeting we had, things clicked," Berman recalled. "I had done a lot of traveling in the '70s working for the United Nations and he had done traveling when he had been a Pan American airline pilot years before. Things just kind of clicked between us."

Roddenberry asked Berman to leave Paramount and work for him on staff. Berman feared that one-hour syndicated TV shows, especially science fiction shows, were a tough sell.

Berman said he made this tough career choice because "There was something very straightforward about Gene. He had a vision of the future that he integrated into STAR TREK twenty-five years prior to my meeting him."

RENE WHAT'S-HIS-NAME...

The actors came on after Berman. Larry King again mispronounced Rene's name, but in a new way! He called him "Rene Auberjonoy," and everybody laughed.

Rene remarked that people turn into Dan Quayle in the headlights when they get to his name. He said he doesn't understand why.

King then asked Rene if he ever considered changing his name for stage purposes. Rene replied, "I did, briefly. I changed it to Fauber, which is my father's first initial and the first five letters of Auberjonois. Then people called me *Reen Fawber.* It doesn't matter. You can't win."

Larry King asked Avery Brooks whether he had to read for the part of Commander Sisko. He replied that he read for the role but didn't think he'd get the part. He said he enjoyed reading for the part, but didn't get his hopes up because others were also reading for the role.

"I was thrilled. I was stunned by the story and pilot, and that's why I proceeded. My wife kept saying, 'Avery, just don't say no.'" Rick Berman confirmed that a number of people read for the part but they felt their search had ended when Avery read for it.

Nana Visitor explained that she landed the role of Kira Nerys following two five minute auditions. "I came in for the producers and came back and did it again for Paramount, and that was it. It was one of the quickest processes I've ever been through," she recalled.

When she got the script from her agent she didn't read the cover page. She didn't realize she was reading for STAR TREK. She just read the Major Kira scenes and was so impressed that she felt she had to get the part.

She said, "First of all it was the writing. It's hard to find writing like this. It's everything an actor wants to play with, you know? It makes it Disneyland.

"This woman was multidimensional and fallible and opinionated and all these things that are so rich. How wonderful playing someone who has somewhere to go; some kind of growth. It has to happen in her life."

Rene Auberjonois was appearing in the play "City of Angels" when the script for DEEP SPACE NINE came through. "I'd love to say they just offered it to me, but that's not true," he said.

He had to do several readings for the producers. He continued, "I think partly because the character is a very complex character that could have been cast with a number of different actors. A woman could have played this character Odo. I read it and, again, I was blown away by it."

He said he talked about the part with his family at dinner the night he read for the role. His daughter was sure he'd get the part. "Then I proceeded to go through a series of auditions in which Rick (Berman) was one of my strongest supporters," he recalled, "but (he) had to convince some other people."

Berman confirmed that there were three Paramount production people who also had to approve the major actors cast in the series.

Avery Brooks explained that when he was going to direct the DEEP SPACE NINE episode "Tribunal," he saw that Fritz Weaver was going to come in to read for a part. He was flabbergasted because he knew exactly who Fritz Weaver was. The man has been a professional actor for some thirty years.

Larry King wanted to understand the concept behind auditioning. He asked Nana Visitor if after DEEP SPACE NINE has run its course for eight years or so she would still be willing to read for parts. She replied, "I am one of those people who like to audition. It's like, watch this and tell me what you think because if you don't like it then I don't want to do it."

Rene explained, "It just depends on what the project is. You've got to understand that (with) STAR TREK, every actor in this city, New York, Chicago (and) London was trying to get on this show."

Nana Visitor said science fiction is popular "because it deals with a lot of the same issues that we deal with in our lives, and yet it's once removed. We can sit back and look at it and not feel threatened, and experience things that we need to."

Larry King pointed out that science fiction television has not been successful. Rick Berman observed, "Even the original STAR TREK flopped. In a way, THE NEXT GENERATION is one of the first science fiction weekly series that's been successful."

PRESSURE

Demands are put on science fiction that are not put on other genres of television shows. Berman explained, "I think our audience is very demanding in terms of what they're expecting from our shows. I think we try to be thought-provoking. We try to deal with issues. With any good science fiction you take an issue and you turn it on its ear a little bit and look at it from a different perspective.

"STAR TREK fans take this all very seriously. They expect the best from us and that's what we have to give them weekly."

Rene described fan expectations saying fans ask, "Is it science fiction? Is it fantasy?

"It is mythology and it speaks to something very, very deep in people, and not even Eurocentric mythology. The audience has an investment in it.

"A lot of people don't. I've had friends who sit and watch it and go, 'What are you talking about?' They don't know what it's about. Then I get letters from professors at M.I.T. or a ten year old kid on a farm in Iowa, so the demographic is so broad."

Avery Brooks added, "I couldn't agree more. There's this notion of contemporary mythology, and things hoped for; the evidence of things not seen."

Brooks related his experience working on the pilot standing in front of a blue screen that will later contain special effects. The effects will eventually surround the actor and he will seem to be reacting to them.

Brooks said, "I started to laugh hysterically. I'm sitting in a room and you are literally alone on this screen. I'm sitting in the middle of the floor, with eighty people standing around, sinking into some place. I realized two things. One, how absurd it all is. The other is that I could do this all day long.

"You surrender yourself to it. It is this thing we do. We are talking about a glimpse of the infinite. We are talking about something high-fallutin', this thing called art. That's what we do, try to touch somebody."

Larry King recalled that Isaac Asimov once told him that, to the reader, science fiction must be believable. Nana Visitor explained that after working on the set for 17 hours, the starfield backdrop becomes absolutely real to her. She said, "I'm there. I'm out in space. I do have a nose that looks like this. Absolutely real. On the pilot it took 17 hours (a day), but it doesn't take that long now."

"I think it frees you in ways," Rene added. "After all we are children who are making a living instead of saying to our parents in the living room after dinner, watch me do a play, watch me do a play. We are now doing it for millions of people, and it frees us, too."

Rick Berman said that a DEEP SPACE NINE movie will be done in a few years. Avery revealed that none of the DEEP SPACE NINE actors will appear in the NEXT GENERATION movie.

This isn't unexpected. STAR TREK—GENERATIONS already has many people in the cast. To have included any of the actors from DEEP SPACE NINE would have reduced them to a simple cameo appearance.

One rumor says DEEP SPACE NINE isn't successful. It was put to rest when Larry King asked producer Rick Berman, who replied that the series is extremely successful. He said, "It's doing as well as THE NEXT GENERATION did in its second year and getting better all the time."

THE RIGHT WORDS

Rene was asked if he had script approval. They discussed the complicated process undertaken when an actor wants to change a line.

He said, "A lot of television is written by committee. If I turn to the script person and say, 'I'm going to say this instead of that,' and if it's generally the same thing, fine. You don't do that with STAR TREK. If you're going to change a word, and sometimes it gets on your nerves as an actor, you go to the script person and say, 'I think it would be better if I said it this way.'

"Then they go to the phone and they call up and they talk to Rick or Michael Piller or somebody up there. Then you get the word back if it's all right or it's not all right, and you go on. Most of the time it is (all right)."

Berman says it's always difficult to get good scripts. He noted, "Finding good writers and finding good scripts and keeping people interested and keeping people involved is always the key to making it work."

Avery Brooks said he asked to direct "Tribunal." He recalled, "I should have made this turn a long time ago. They were gracious enough to let me do this.

"Directing is something that I've been doing in theatre for a long time. Doing it now in this electronic medium is something that I must do."

Avery Brooks is the director of the National Black Arts Festival. He explained, "It began in 1988 and this is the fourth largest bi-annual festival which celebrates the culture of African Americans and people of African descent."

He continued by noting "there are eight disciplines, including music, dance and we can go on and on. We talk about health as well. This is the only one of its kind in the world where you have this serious discussion of the presence of African people in the world. It's the only one that I'm aware of unless somebody writes in and tells me where there is another one.

"I'm Artistic Director. I gather them and set it loose. The culture speaks. It's a wonderful thing."

Nana Visitor admitted she had been in some bombs. She said she was "in Broadway bombs."

She continued, "I closed a lot of shows in Boston. It's awful. It's like losing a friend. You have such high hopes and you think it's going to be a hit and you'll be working.

"That's the main thing. Oh my God, I've got to go back to auditioning! I was dancing in shows then."

She admitted she missed dancing. She doesn't expect to dance professionally again.

She said, "My mother still teaches. She's going to be eighty in May and she still teaches. I will go to her class when I'm there for her birthday, but otherwise it's too painful. I'm out of it now. I won't go back."

She explained that working on the series full time keeps her from any other activities. She also has a two year old child that she's raising.

Rene said that the best thing about being on a successful series is that he can go home at night rather than having to travel in a play. He said, "I must say that I've really been blessed by this business. Here in this city when I did BENSON for six years, my kids were at an age where I was able to get up in the morning and make them breakfast and make them lunch and drive them to school and have a life and now they're off in college."

He revealed that he's in the same situation as Nana Visitor. He has been appearing in a play where he's at a restaurant at the opening night party and suddenly realizes that the whole room has cleared out because the early reviews have come in and the play will be closing immediately.

Rick Berman said television critics can affect the success of a TV show. The producer admitted, "To some degree; nowhere near to the degree that it does on Broadway or even on a motion picture." Television is a free medium and even TV shows which are universally panned such as THE FACTS OF LIFE or THREE'S COMPANY can still become top rated shows and run for years.

On the other hand, some shows that are universally praised, such as PICKET FENCES, don't do well. Reviews seem to have no effect on TV ratings.

TAKE STAR TREK SERIOUSLY

Larry King suggested doing a talk show in space. Avery Brooks pointed out that it's a mistake to joke about STAR TREK because it is taken seriously by its viewers.

"Rene talked about it earlier," he said. "I mean on a certain level we can ha-ha about it, but you really do have to call across the lot about it all."

"You have to be serious about something that's potentially so silly," Berman explained. "There's people with funny make-up on their face flying around at speeds faster than the speed of light, running into other humanoid people who happen to speak English very well. We all take it very, very seriously. I think that that's what's kept the show as clear."

"There's a big difference between reality and truth," Rene said. "What we are is true, and it doesn't matter whether it's fantastical. The audience recognizes it as coming from a true place."

"The key to our series are these people, are the characters," Berman continued. "Good science fiction on television has to be character driven and these people represent, with their colleagues, two families of explorers."

DEEP SPACE

The Characters

LT. JADZIA DAX

Jadzia Dax is a Trill. Trills consist of two entities joined in a symbiotic relationship. The external humanoid form, Jadzia, is a beautiful young woman of twenty-eight. She possesses great intelligence and charm. The symbiont, Dax, is a three hundred year old sluglike being every bit as intelligent as its host.

Jadzia is Dax's seventh host. Jadzia and Dax combine all knowledge, memories and wisdom. This includes Dax's recollections of a twenty-year friendship with Commander Benjamin Sisko while living in its previous host, Curzon.

This is a symbiotic relationship. Both personalities merge and interact. Each pairing creates a new person and continues the life of the slug.

A slug undergoes diverse experiences while living in a series of host bodies. During his pairings, Dax has fathered two children and given birth to three. Curzon Dax was both mentor and friend to young Benjamin Sisko. Sisko still sometimes addresses Jadzia Dax as "old man" despite the recent switch in gender.

Many hundreds of years ago, the invertebrate, androgynous, sluglike symbionts lived separate from humanoids. They dwelt in a subterranean realm. Humanoids lived on the surface of their planet.

A major environmental disaster forced the species to work together. The relationship became symbiotic. The slugs could not live on the surface without a host.

Not every humanoid becomes a host. Most live as single entities. The humanoids outnumber the slugs. Once a humanoid unites with a slug they create one coherent personality from two distinct components.

JADZIA DAX

When Curzon died, Dax moved to Jadzia's body through a surgical procedure. Dax lives in her abdominal cavity. Jadzia wanted to host a slug since she was a child.

Jadzia was one of the top candidates of this difficult job. She underwent long, arduous training. Mental, psychological and physical tests discerned if she her qualifications to serve as a host. She excelled.

She proved unparalleled in the academic world. Long before she joined Dax, she earned doctoral degrees in a variety of scientific fields, including zoology, astrophysics, exoarchaeology and exobiology. Dax added generations of scientific knowledge. Jadzia Dax, the combined entity, is an expert in an astounding array of fields, technical, cultural and scientific.

THE SECRET IN SPACE
Jadzia Dax arrived at Deep Space Nine shortly after Commander Benjamin Sisko took charge. A new volunteer doctor on the station, Julian Bashir, soon began flirting with the attractive, young woman.

Dax and Sisko renewed their friendship. When the Trill examined the mysterious Orb Sisko brought back from Bajor, the alien artifact triggered a vivid recollection of the transfer of Dax from the dying Curzon to her.

Jadzia Dax joined Sisko on a dangerous mission to the Denorios Belt, the area near Bajor where the orbs were found. They found the opening of a wormhole and were soon drawn into its vortex.

Dax discovered they had entered the Gamma Quadrant. They stepped back through the wormhole into a strange alien landscape.

The orb enveloped Dax, carrying her back to the station. It left Sisko behind. Ever the scientist, Dax returned to work immediately. She played a crucial role forestalling the Cardassians while helping Chief Miles O'Brien move the space station near the wormhole.

PAST MASTER
Alien intruders once tried to kidnap Jadzia Dax. The attempted abduction opened a can of worms. Curzon Dax had fought in the civil war on the planet Klaestron.

General Ardelon Tandro became a martyr around whose memory the winning side rallied. When Sisko captured Dax's escaping abductors, one was Tandro's son, Ilon. That implicated Curzon Dax as the murderer of the famed general. Ilon wanted to extradite Dax for trial. The Bajorans had no extradition arrangements with the Klaestrons, longtime allies of the Cardassians.

A hearing determined if Dax would be removed. It also judged whether Jadzia Dax was accountable for the actions of Curzon Dax.

Jadzia remained silent about the charges. This puzzled Sisko. He couldn't pry information from his old friend.

Odo investigated Klaestron and discovered that Curzon Dax had been a friend of the dead General, and the dead general's widow, Enina. She refuted the notion that Dax killed her husband. She said her son was unduly obsessed with his dead father. Then she discovered Curzon Dax missing, and that Dax had merged with Jadzia.

The behavior of Jadzia Dax proves perplexing. She says nothing about the accusations. Sisko defends Curzon Dax. Fascinating philosophical questions about the nature of the Trill emerge. The real drama begins when Odo says that Curzon Dax and Enina Tando had an affair. Dax reluctantly admits the truth, but refuses to speak about it publicly. Dax will not do anything to damage the reputation of the woman Curzon Dax loved.

The debate raged, and Ilon seemed on the verge of victory. Then his own mother interrupted the proceedings to provide Curzon Dax with an alibi: he was with her. Curzon Dax had sworn to keep this secret to protect the reputations of Enina and General Tandro. The people of Klaestron need not know the truth about their great hero.

General Tandro had died trying to betray his own side!

MASTER OF THE GAME

Jadzia Dax is intriguing. She has many interests, but her hobby is foiling the amorous intentions of Dr. Julian Bashir. Dr. Julian Bashir is obsessed with winning her. She is amused, even if somewhat attracted.

She's been a man herself, which takes some of the mystery out of sex for her. She is particularly amused when Julian Bashir's ideal version of her—crazy about him, somewhat vacant, utterly submissive— becomes an actual entity. This Jadzia Dax becomes annoying after a while. The real Jadzia Dax, and the embarrassed Bashir, are relieved when she disappears. This helped Julian understand that his vision of Dax is quite different from the real Dax. His amorous attentions have since moved elsewhere.

Julian once approached Jadzia while she was meditating while playing an Altonian Brain-Teaser. The doctor couldn't keep the bubble-like sphere supported with calm. This would have resulted in complete control of the neural Theta waves that produce the sphere.

When the sphere lost its integrity after transferring from Dax to Bashir, Jadzia comforted the doctor. She told Julian she practiced the game for 140 years.

Julian noted that Dax had cold hands. She admitted this was a peculiarity of the Trill, to which Julian responded, "Cold hands, warm heart."

Julian trusted Jadzia with his personal diaries. Dax confessed that she had not read the journals when Julian and Miles were believed killed. Kira suggested she keep them.

DAX AND MILES

Jadzia Dax and Miles O'Brien respect each other as Starfleet officers. O'Brien is bemused that Dax has both hundreds of years of experience and a body that distracts young ensigns.

He enjoys Dax's sense of humor but fails to understand why she wastes time playing cards with Quark and his Ferengi companions. Dax patiently explained the reasons, but it made no sense to O'Brien. O'Brien does not trust Ferengi.

Dax's competence and calm during crisis please O'Brien. Dax helped O'Brien foil the computer lockouts of an assassination plot against Vedek Barielto.

THE OTHER ALIEN

Dax and Odo share more in common than others on Deep Space Nine. Both differ from other humanoids. The shape shifter Odo possesses unique physical abilities. The ancient Dax possesses wisdom other crewmates cannot achieve. She finds solutions that stymie the logic of the short-lived. Dax and Odo never romantically link but they do enjoy a comradeship that transcends their individual species.

The most harrowing event of Jadzia's life occurred when a disgruntled Trill hijacked the station. The Trill moved Dax from Jadzia's body into his own.

The unbalanced Trill couldn't cope with the change. Sisko eventually stunned him and returned Dax to Jadzia.

Jadzia Dax is fascinating. The beautiful young woman possesses three hundred years of accumulated wisdom. When her life ends, many years from now, Dax will find a new host and always remember the life with Jadzia.

DR. JULIAN BASHIR

by Kay Doty

*D*uring the early episodes of DEEP SPACE NINE many fans were not happy with Siddig El Fadil's space station doctor. He was young, handsome, brash, naive, adventurous and filled with excitement at being ". . . out on the frontier." He loved women.

Many fans wanted a staid, dignified doctor's demeanor just as they wanted an Enterprise in their STAR TREK. DEEP SPACE NINE became a fan favorite without either of them. Julian Bashir didn't fit preconceived notions of an outer space doctor, but he gained a large following including several fan clubs.

Prior to Bashir, Starfleet physicians were middle aged and respectable. Bashir was 27 and looked younger.

He is the only Federation officer who requested assignment to the space station. El Fadil has tempered Bashir's early wide-eyed nature by allowing him to mature while not destroying his joy for living and working in the far reaches of space.

The young medical officer quickly found the adventure he craved. He unexpectedly engaged in conversation with the Cardassian tailor Garak while having lunch in the station Promenade Replimat in "Past Prologue."

EXPERIENCE TEACHES

Unaware Cardassians frequently speak in riddles, Bashir believed Garak was a spy. He rushed the information to Commander Sisko. Sisko had other worries. Two Klingon malcontents, the sisters Lursa and B'Etor of the House of Duras, arrived almost at the same time as Tahna, a former Bajoran terrorist.

Bashir soon found himself involved in an intrigue with the Cardassian. They eventually helped reveal a plot by Tahna to drive the Federation out using bomb elements bought from the Duras sisters.

Chastened by the potentially disastrous events, Bashir's exuberance was temporarily dampened. He had learned adventure could prove to be deadly.

Bashir is gregarious by nature. He chatters away unaware of irritating his fellow officers. The others respect his ability as a doctor but dismiss his suggestions outside his field.

An example occurs in "Armageddon Game." Bashir and Chief O'Brien go to T'Lani Three to assist Kellerun and T'Lani scientists. They want to destroy the biomechanical gene disrupters. The terrifying weapons were used by both races in centuries of war.

The Federation officers succeed and want to celebrate. They are fired on by Kellerun soldiers before they can return to Deep Space Nine. The soldiers believe everyone with knowledge of the weapon's formulas must be killed. This includes Bashir and O'Brien.

FACING DEATH TOGETHER
The two escape, but a few drops of the Harvester fluid spills on O'Brien's arm during the fight. Bashir and O'Brien transport to an old command post on the planet. They find food packets, medical supplies and a discarded communications system in an abandoned building.

O'Brien repairs the system while Bashir unsuccessfully tries to help. The spilled Harvester fluid begins to effect the Chief. O'Brien becomes feverish and soon had problems standing or focusing his eyes.

A new, take-charge Bashir emerges. He orders O'Brien to sit and explain what needs to be done. Bashir sets to work, his giddiness now gone. El Fadil brings maturity to his character that was only glimpsed previously.

Bashir repairs the equipment. They are found by T'Lani and Kellerun forces. When they are about to be executed, Bashir helps the desperately ill Chief to his feet and apologizes for failing to save them.

O'Brien tells the distraught doctor he did his best, adding, "It's been an honor serving with you." An instant later the Ganges transporter seizes the two, removing them from danger.

Later O'Brien is recuperates in the infirmary. His wife Keiko is at his side. Bashir tries to tell the Chief of Operations how much his earlier statement means to him as an embarrassed Chief merely waves him away.

NEW CHARACTER FACETS   Bashir appears briefly melancholy in this episode as he talks of the girl he loves and left behind. He believed marriage and a Starfleet career are incompatible. He then loses some of the ground he'd won into the Chief's good graces by tactlessly repeating gossip about problems in the O'Brien marriage.

Bashir shows compassion for others, a trait shared with his fellow STAR TREK doctors. Like his predecessors, Bashir fights to save lives even when that being is a threat to his own life or the safety of the station. Outstanding examples of Bashir's compassion appear in the second season episodes, "Melora" and "The Wire."

In "Melora," a young ensign, Melora Pazlar, a native of the low gravity planet Elaysia, is temporarily assigned to the space station. The difference in gravity on Deep Space Nine forces Melora to either use a wheelchair or walking aids.

Bashir is attracted to her, but she holds him, and the other station personnel, at arm's length with her barbed comments. The doctor is not put off. He confronts her with the suggestion that this is her, ". . . way of keeping the rest of the universe on the defensive." She thaws enough to accept his dinner invitation.

JULIAN BASHIR

CRITICAL CHOICES
Later Melora invites him to her quarters and turns off the gravity controls. They float toward the ceiling and kiss. Bashir, concerned about her efforts to function in normal gravity, later tells her of a surgical process to allow her to move about without artificial devices.

She feels attraction to the handsome doctor and agrees to consider the experimental procedures. Later, while on an off-station mission, Melora discusses the ramifications of marriage between Starfleet officers with Dax.

The following day, while on another assignment with Dax, thief Fallit Kot forces his way into their runabout. He demands to be taken into the wormhole. An injured and desperate Melora prevents the escape.

After returning to the space station, she dines with Julian. She tells him she will not continue the treatment because it will prevent her ever returning to her home world for long.

Bashir understands but is disappointed. The episode ends on a bittersweet note as the pair hold hands while the Klingon chef sings a love song.

BRASH BUT DIRECT
Bashir has a different problem in "The Wire." His friend Garak will die if he can't find a way to save him.

A device was implanted in Garak's head during the Cardassian occupation of Bajor. No one knows the reason. Now Garak will die if the device cannot safely be removed.

Bashir takes matters into his own hands after Garak refuses to cooperate. Bashir goes on a dangerous journey to Cardassia to confront the one man who can provide the answer to save his friend.

Bashir crashes uninvited into the Cardassian's home and makes demands. The Cardassian is impressed by Bashir's impudence. The man, Garak's former commander, suggests the doctor allow Garak to die. Bashir persists and is given the information he needs.

From the moment Bashir arrived on Deep Space Nine, he unintentionally offended and irritated nearly everyone. Fresh out of medical school, after a comfortable and protected childhood, he felt so much excitement and awe in his first Starfleet post that it never occurs to him not everyone shares his enthusiasm.

Bashir considers Chief O'Brien his best friend. The Chief of Operations grumbles publicly but secretly admits there is substance to Bashir.

El Fadil gives Bashir strength of character. It allows him to brush aside the many insults that come his way from fellow officers as he slowly gains their respect and friendship.

DISCOVERED ON PBS
Twenty-four year old Siddig El Fadil came to DEEP SPACE NINE with less acting experience than his cast mates, with the possible exceptions of Cirroc Lofton and Aron Eisenberg. He wasn't sure he wanted to be an actor as his interests lay in directing.

Many out-of-work actors take jobs waiting tables or moving furniture. Out-of-work directors must also find other work while waiting for their big break. El Fadil was fortunate. He found his acting.

After several bit parts in miscellaneous productions, he was cast as the aged King Faisel in the British produced A DANGEROUS MAN—LAWRENCE AFTER ARABIA. Carried on PBS in the United States, the six-part mini-series was a critical disappointment, but provided the break Siddig needed. DEEP SPACE NINE Executive Producer Rick Berman saw the series.

Berman liked El Fadil's performance and considered him for the role of Sisko. Then he learned that the actor was in his mid-twenties, so he cast him as the doctor.

El Fadil is fun to watch. He takes his space-illiterate character along a bumpy road adjusting to his surroundings, fellow officers and the very real dangers of life on a space station.

MAJOR KIRA NERYS

by Kay Doty

"Emissary," the two-hour movie that kicked off DEEP SPACE NINE, introduced an angry, unhappy Major Kira Nerys, played by Nana Visitor. Kira had fought for a dream most of her life

It had finally become reality — the hated Cardassians were evacuating her home world of Bajor! They were abandoning their space station as well. Just when Kira should have been ecstatic, she was outraged by the actions of her own leaders.

The Bajoran Provisional Government requested the assistance of the Federation in administering the space station. Kira passionately believed Bajorans could run the station without outside help.

When Starfleet Commander Benjamin Sisko arrived to assume command, Kira was openly hostile and frequently insubordinate. Nana Visitor convincingly portrayed the anger and frustration of her character.

CHARACTERIZATION
The seasoned actress could easily have maintained the strong negative emotions to the exclusion of all others. Kira would have become a one dimensional boring character. Visitor did not do that.

Visitor had been a working actress for several years when the show began, but her name was hardly a household word. DEEP SPACE NINE changed that. Visitor resisted the temptation to slip into the background of the large ensemble. Instead, Major Kira always causes fireworks.

Major Kira and Lieutenant Jadzia Dax offer strong female role models in a medium sadly lacking in them. The serene Dax maintains an internal calm, perhaps a factor of her extreme age. Kira is volatile. Her emotions quickly change. She does nothing by halves.

One such abrupt change in temperament occurs in "Duet." Events force her to examine her motives.

Cardassian Aamin Marritza arrives at the station. Kira learns he suffers from Kalla-Nohra syndrome. She knows he must have contacted the illness during a mining accident at Gallitepp, the worst forced labor camp on Bajor during the occupation. She is horrified.

Although Marritza was a lowly file clerk, she wants him returned to Bajor for trial. Her demands escalate when evidence indicates he might be the cruel Gallitepp commandant, Gul Darhe'el.

The prisoner tells Kira, "It's not the truth you're interested in — all you want is vengeance." The comment strikes a nerve.

CHANGE
An investigation proves the Cardassian is a file clerk surgically altered to look like Gul Darhe'el. He considers himself a coward who covered his ears to shut out the cries of tortured and dying Bajorans.

When Kira learns Marritza had tried to rescue Bajorans from forced labor camps, her anger dies. He believed a public trial would force Cardassia to admit its guilt.

A different Kira emerges as the truth slowly appears. Her anger dissolves into understanding and pity as she listens to his tearful confession. She releases him from his cell, telling him he is a good man and there will be no trial.

A grateful Kira tries to help him come to terms with his feelings of guilt for events he could not control. "What you tried to do was very honorable," she says. "If Cardassia is going to change it's going to need people like you."

Her compassion later turns to grief. Marritza dies in her arms, stabbed to death by a renegade Bajoran, a survivor of Gallitepp.

Visitor gradually softened Kira, allowing her an occasional smile. She began to accept the presence of the Federation with good grace, at least most of the time. Kira learned Sisko isn't an ogre.

Habits formed over a lifetime die hard. It is unlikely she'll ever become complacent or completely control her emotions towards Bajor.

A CIRCLE OF FRIENDS

In the second season's opening episode, "The Homecoming," she is relieved of duty by the Bajoran Minister Jaro. Several fellow officers express outrage at her dismissal and meek acceptance. Even Quark joins the party in "The Circle."

When her own people kidnap her from the monastery, hold her prisoner and torture her, she is rescued by Starfleet officers. A contrite Kira re-evaluates her opinion of Federation officers.

As the second season progressed, Kira learned to trust Starfleet officers. A part of her still looks forward to the day they leave and Bajor gains complete control of the station.

Kira is surprised to discover Vedek Bareil (Philip Anglim) has a romantic interest in her. She is even more surprised to learn she harbors similar feelings for him. She refuses to acknowledge this attraction, even to herself.

Everything changes in "Shadowplay" when Quark invites Bareil to the station. Quark hopes Bareil will divert Kira so he can conduct his nefarious business. After she catches Quark, she thanks him for bringing the Vedek to the station. Kira and Bareil acknowledge their growing affection for each other.

SHADOW FROM THE PAST

The relationship is tested before the election of a new Kai in "The Collaborator." The ambitious Vedek Winn provides evidence suggesting that Vedek Bareil collaborated with the Cardassians during the occupation. Winn challenges Kira to learn the truth.

When Kira finds evidence against Bareil, she is devastated. She tells Odo she loves Bareil.

Confronted with altered records, Bareil removes his name from the list of candidates. Winn is elected Kai.

The unhappy Kira refuses to believe her own findings. She searches further, discovering that Bareil could not have been the collaborator. He has been covering for someone else. He admits the truth but extracts a promise that she keep his secret.

"What about us?" he asks. She kisses him in reply. Hand in hand they go to pay their respects to the new Kai.

It will be interesting to see how this relationship develops. Continuing romance has never been part of a STAR TREK series.

THE DARK SIDE

Perhaps Visitor's most challenging episode was her dual role in "Crossover," when she and Dr. Bashir found themselves in a parallel universe. Although the parallel universe contained duplicates of Sisko, Odo, O'Brien and Garak, Kira was the only one who had to confront herself.

Kira Nerys was desperate to return home, and is afraid of her "twin." Intendent Kira, commander of the station, was delighted by the course of events. The Intendent smiled, laughed and was enchanted by her look-alike. Kira eventually found a way home with the help of Bashir and people from the parallel universe.

Visitor played two very different roles perfectly, supplying each with the proper emotions. It is Visitor's best episode.

Kira now shows compassion, joy and sadness. In "Armageddon Game," she demonstrates grief when she believes O'Brien and Bashir have been killed. The hard anger of her early days has dissipated but still bubbles just below the surface.

Major Kira Nerys is the strongest female character ever to appear regularly on STAR TREK, perhaps on any television series. Good scripts and directors play a part in this success, but most of the credit must go to Nana Visitor. She gave Kira a vibrant, multifaceted personality.

CHIEF OBRIEN

by Kay Doty

Colm Meaney's Chief O'Brien is the only regular character to serve on THE NEXT GENERATION before transferring to DEEP SPACE NINE. O'Brien was already familiar to STAR TREK fans when the new series began.

Actor Meaney began life in outer space as the Conn Ensign in "Encounter At Farpoint," THE NEXT GENERATION's two-hour pilot. He was a security guard in "Lonely Among Us," but did not become the ship's transporter chief until the second season opener, "The Child." In that role his main action consisted of beaming people on to and off the ship. His character didn't have a name until well into the second season.

O'Brien waited two years before he gained first and middle names, Miles Edward. That same season gave the character a bride and made him a hero in back-to-back episodes "Data's Day" and "The Wounded."

THE EARLY DAYS
The early roles gave Meaney scant opportunity to develop his character. He first began to grow in "Data's Day" and "The Wounded."

"Data's Day" presented him as a typical nervous bridegroom. He was first angry, then bewildered when his equally nervous bride-to-be canceled the wedding then reconsidered and went on with the ceremony. Many husbands and wives empathized with the bridal pair in "Data's Day."

In "The Wounded," he almost single-handedly prevented a Federation-Cardassian war. He persuaded his former commander, a near insane Captain Maxwell, that a Cardassian task force meant the Federation no harm. O'Brien was not convinced of the truth of his own statement.

A poignant scene occurred in "The Wounded" between Maxwell and O'Brien when they shared a few bars from a simple song, a memento of past service together. It showcased the Irish actor's talents.

Before departing THE NEXT GENERATION to join DEEP SPACE NINE at the end of the fifth season, O'Brien became a father in "Disaster." He also became a villain in "Power Play."

SPOTLIGHT ON O'BRIEN   A power failure resulted in a shutdown of nearly all systems in "Disaster." O'Brien and Ensign Ro find themselves alone on the bridge with an uncertain Counselor Troi. Troi, as the senior officer present, assumes command.

Ro insists, almost to the point of insubordination, that Troi order an immediate separation of the saucer section. A hesitant O'Brien points out that there could be survivors in engineering working on the problem.

O'Brien worried about his immediately expectant wife, Keiko. A reluctant Worf played midwife in a hilarious scene.

Meaney personifies evil in "Power Play." Alien entities possess O'Brien, Troi and Data. They want to use their bodies to escape from a penal colony on Mab-Bu VI.

All three actors excellently portray roles very different from their regular characters. The normally placid O'Brien menaces his wife and newborn child. This episode dispelled any remaining doubts about Meaney's acting abilities.

Meaney's popularity with STAR TREK fans grew steadily. Meaney/O'Brien brought a built-in following to DEEP SPACE NINE's premiere episode, "Emissary," in January 1993. He was not deemed important enough to be included in the NEXT GENERATION publicity photos, but now plays an integral member of the DEEP SPACE NINE ensemble.

THE DEMANDS OF THE JOB

The newly promoted Chief of Operations brought 22 years of Starfleet experience to his post on Deep Space Nine. He had his hands full keeping the space station from falling apart.

He had to return all systems to active status, including deciphering Cardassian codes and instructions. He also had to become acclimated to his new assignment on a run down space station after years on the pristine Enterprise.

His personal life also offered challenges. He learned to cope with a new and very different commanding officer and a wife who hated being on the space station.

Meaney gave an excellent performance. O'Brien was clearly a man with too much to do, too many people demanding his attention, and far too little time to accomplish near impossible tasks. Congenial, happy-go-lucky O'Brien is also a devoted father and husband with a good sense of humor.

Bickering between Spock and McCoy is a beloved feature of the original STAR TREK series. Banter never developed between characters in THE NEXT GENERATION. DEEP SPACE NINE is twice-blessed with both Quark's bickering with Odo and the conflict between Bashir and O'Brien.

Meaney convincingly runs a gantlet of emotions during DEEP SPACE NINE's first two seasons. He exhibits compassion for a young Cardassian boy torn between his adoptive Bajoran parents and Cardassian father in "Cardassians" and for the hunted Tosk in "Captive Pursuit." He displays anger and bewilderment in "Whispers" and "The Siege," and humor in "The Storyteller."

AN ODD COUPLE

"The Storyteller" finds O'Brien assigned to chauffeur Dr. Bashir on an emergency medical mission to a small Bajoran village. Bashir tries to get better acquainted with the Chief, urging the annoyed O'Brien to call him Julian.

The dying village Sirah names the Chief his successor. The Chief is told that a horrible creature, the Dal'Rok, will destroy the village by nightfall. It is up to Sirah O'Brien to save them.

O'Brien doesn't intend to spend the rest of his life in the village. He hasn't the slightest idea how to escape his fate and is particularly displeased when three young Bajoran women are ushered into his room. When he asked what he could do for them, Bashir smirks, "I think they want to do something for you."

O'Brien and Bashir unsuccessfully try to learn the secret of the Dal'Rok. They are interrupted when Hovath, the rightful Sirah heir whom the villagers refuse to accept, attempts to murder O'Brien.

As the Dal'Rok again approaches, O'Brien tries to tell the story. The villagers cower in fear when Hovath steps in and tells the story, driving off the Dal'Rok. The villagers belatedly realize Hovath is their true Sirah.

As the two officers return to the space station, Bashir tells a relieved O'Brien that he doesn't have to call him Julian until he is ready.

This episode is essentially a comedy. Nog and Jake add fun by annoying Odo, who shows no sense of humor in this instance.

The first season's "Captive Pursuit" demonstrates a compassionate side of O'Brien's nature. He risks everything, including his commission, to help the hunted Tosk elude his captors.

A DOUBLE LIFE   "Whispers" is an O'Brien vehicle. Other cast members are little more than extras.

O'Brien returns from the Parada System after a week of briefings for the upcoming peace talks to be held at Deep Space Nine. He finds things not quite what they should be.

He discovers a subordinate doing his work under Sisko's orders, is forced to undergo a lengthy physical examination by Sisko's orders, and is then restricted from secure areas he himself established. Sisko assigns him "busy" work far from vital areas of the station. His fellow officers act strangely, and so do his wife and daughter.

O'Brien wonders if he is seriously ill until Bashir gives him a clean bill of health. He speculates that the odd activities denote a surprise birthday party, except his birthday remains months away.

The Chief suspects the unthinkable, a conspiracy. After stealing a runabout, he contacts Starfleet only to be ordered back to the station.

A thoroughly confused O'Brien returns to the Parada System in search of answers. He is attacked and mortally wounded by phaser fire after beaming down to the surface.

Of course, this isn't the real O'Brien. A replicant had been programmed to believe he is O'Brien and disrupt the forthcoming peace talks. The real O'Brien had been kidnapped. He was not rescued until after the replicant escaped from Deep Space Nine.

This episode gave Meaney the opportunity to display a wide range of emotions. He made the most of it, showing pain at his family's rejection, anger at the thought of a widespread conspiracy, fear, confusion and frustration. He delivers an excellent performance.

ANOTHER SIDE

An entirely different O'Brien appears in "Crossover," the parallel universe episode. All Terrans are slaves in this universe. O'Brien is a hopeless tinkerer and putterer living in constant fear of punishment over the smallest, unintended, infraction of the rules.

Bashir and Kira terrify the parallel O'Brien. They accidentally arrive in his world, asking his help to return home. He reluctantly agrees to help. When they are caught and questioned by the station commander, Kira's double, his reply to her question why he would want to escape is, ". . . anything has to be better than this."

The versatile Meaney plays each of O'Brien's relationships with his fellow officers differently yet consistent with the show. He is a character actor with talents similar to those of his co-star, Rene Auberjonois.

Colm Meaney isn't young and attractive like Siddig El Faddil or fortyish and handsome like Avery Brooks. He is an average looking guy playing an average guy doing a blue collar job. He keeps things running, and is often up to his elbows in repair and maintenance work.

A FAMILY MAN
He is the only main character with a wife and child. Sisko is a family man, but his wife is dead.

Miles O'Brien is a regular guy with a tough job, a family to support and all the pressures that accompany it. When he gets involved in extraordinary situations, he has to consider his family. It is surprising when he embarks on hazardous missions. In "Homecoming" he accompanies Major Kira on a perilous rescue mission and in "The Jem 'Hedar" he takes part in another rescue mission, this time to retrieve Sisko, Quark, Jake and Nog. O'Brien piloted the rescue ship that retrieved his commander.

These are risky activities for a family man with a vital job on the space station. O'Brien knows the inner workings of the station. He could be described as the most essential person on the ship except for Commander Sisko. He should be in charge when Sisko is off station.

O'Brien makes sure everything works. He lacks the youth and attractiveness of some cast members, but his character has been explored more deeply and regularly than anyone except Major Kira.

ODO

Security chief Odo's origins are shrouded in mystery. He was discovered adrift in a spaceship fifty years before the arrival of the Federation at Deep Space Nine. He possessed no memory of his past. The Bajorans who discovered him in the Denorios asteroid belt named him Odo.

Odo lived on Bajor for many years. He can transform himself into any object. Many regard him as a freak. This may account for his grim, isolated personality.

He opted to take a humanoid form to function among Bajorans and Cardassians. He is not a humanoid at all, but a shapeless blob. Odo must return to his amorphous state every day or risk serious damage to his health. He spends part of each day in a bucket.

He resents having to take humanoid form. It emerges in humorless cynicism and frequent exasperated observations about the absurd behavior of humanoids.

The Cardassians ruled Bajor and Deep Space Nine with an iron fist. Odo dealt with these authority figures, but isn't fond of them. He does appreciate the Cardassian desire for order.

LAWMAN
Odo became the head of security on the space station. The head Cardassian, Gul Dukat, trusted him because of his sincere interest in justice and immunity to temptation. Money, food and sex don't interest the shapeshifter.

Gul Dukat risked occasional incidents when Odo's sense of justice conflicted with Cardassian political interests. This was preferable to giving the job to an ambitious Cardassian who could build a power base, and easier than co-opting a Bajoran for the job.

ODO

The Ferengi Quark became the main target of Odo's watchful eye. He is both Odo's adversary and friend. Odo overlooks small infractions by Quark in exchange for his aid.

Quark thinks he gets the better of Odo but Odo often comes out ahead. The relationship is a give and take both relish.

The Federation and Bajorans kept him as security chief on Deep Space Nine. The role appeals to him. When the Cardassians left, they stripped both planet and space station of everything of value. Odo sees himself as the preserver of law and order in the ensuing chaos.

Much to Odo's chagrin, Commander Sisko also asked Quark to stay. Their cat-and-mouse game continues.

Odo prefers working with Sisko and the Federation to the Cardassians. He does sometimes miss that his job was simpler during the Cardassian occupation.

Sisko met Odo shortly after arriving on the station. Odo revealed his amazing shape shifting powers to Sisko when a criminal threw a weapon at him. The criminal remained belligerent so Sisko fired a phaser blast into the air to end the conflict.

Odo astounded Sisko by telling the new Commander no weapons were allowed on the Promenade and promptly confiscating his weapon! Odo doesn't bend rules for anybody, not even his superior officer.

Odo was perplexed by Sisko's desire that Quark remain on board the space station. He soon learned the reason. Odo admired Sisko for ruthlessly using Nog's arrest to force Quark to do his bidding.

Later, when Cardassians renewed their interest in the station, Odo demonstrated his loyalty to the Federation. Disguised as the bag in which "lucky"

Cardassians placed their winnings from Quark's casino, Odo boarded their ship. He disabled their sensor array and other systems, enabling Sisko and Dax to leave without being detected.

ODO AND KIRA
Odo is always pragmatic and often bemused by procedural matters. When Lursa and B'Etor, the Klingon sisters, showed up on Deep Space Nine, Odo forestalled trouble by alerting the Klingon government and handing them over. He is not surprised when Commander Sisko prefers to watch and wait.

Odo and Major Kira Nerys have known each other for a long time. They first met during the Cardassian occupation when Kira was a prime suspect in a murder investigation. Odo never solved the case due to an alibi provided Kira by Quark.

Another case revealed that Kira was on the station as an operative of the Bajoran underground. She had killed the victim in self-defense. Odo's friendship with Kira holds a lingering doubt from this case. It surfaces when they discuss Kira's mixed feelings about another Bajoran undergrounder on the station.

As security chief of Deep Space Nine Odo often deals with freedom fighters cum terrorists. He once informed a middle-aged Bajoran on the Promenade that he had 24 hours to leave the station. When Sisko later questioned Odo's action, Odo explained that the Bajoran was a dubious character from the Bajoran underground. Although regarded as a hero by many, Odo sees him as nothing more than an opportunistic black marketer.

OLD DEBTS
The shapeshifter says the undergrounder once let a girl die because she couldn't afford his price for a black market drug. Later Odo convicted the man of the murder of a Cardassian. When the Cardassians left, the provisional government of Bajor set the "hero" free.

Sisko insisted the undergrounder's presence was not illegal. Odo remained determined to run the man off the station. He insisted, "Laws change depending on who's making them, but justice is justice."

ODO

When the undergrounder was murdered in a holosuite, suspicion fell on Odo. Sisko removed the shape shifter from the investigation. Bajorans on the station were goaded by an unknown, bearded Bajoran to take action against Odo. Some stood with him against mob violence.

Dr. Bashir uncovered the bizarre truth. The undergrounder cloned himself, murdered his clone and left the holosuite. The bearded man was both the perpetrator and the victim. He was unpleasantly surprised when Odo arrested him for killing his own clone.

This story revealed Odo's isolation. Unaware of his own origin, forced to mimic those he lives among, he is alone in the universe with only his moral code to guide him.

He was further isolated when he was one of the few not afflicted by the aphasia virus. When the crisis peaked, Odo had only Quark as his ally. Odo is resourceful and brave.

ODO INVESTIGATES
Odo was challenged by the near abduction of Jadzia Dax by Klaestron intruders. The Klaestron insisted Jadzia be charged with a murder committed by Curzon Dax years earlier. The intruders almost kidnapped Dax off the station right under his nose.

Odo began to suspect that the widow of the murdered man held something back. He examined the communication records and developed the hypothesis that Curzon Dax and this woman had an affair at the time of the murder.

He had turned up a reasonable motive for murder. Once Odo confronted the woman with the theory, she provided Curzon Dax with a perfect alibi. He had been sleeping with her at the time of the murder.

Odo takes his position on Deep Space Nine very seriously. He is loath to surrender authority. He once allowed Starfleet security officer, Lieutenant George Primmin, to take charge of a crucial deuridium shipment to the station.

As Primmin took charge, one of the most compelling mysteries of Odo's career unfolded. Rao Vantaka, a murderer who left a trail of death across the galaxy, arrived on the station. Vantaka was a prisoner of Ty Kajada. He arrived only to die in Doctor Bashir's arms.

Vantaka made trouble anyway. After tracking her prey for 20 years, Ty Kajada was not convinced he was dead. He had convincingly faked his own death many times in the past.

Vantaka had planned to steal the deuridium shipment. Deuridium is particularly valuable to Kobliads, the species to which Kajada and Vantaka belong. It extends their life spans.

The shape shifter had his hands full with Vantaka, Kajada and Primmin. He soon found that all his files had been erased from the computers. His annoyance at Primmin led him to offer his resignation to Sisko. Sisko assured Odo he was still in charge of security on DS9.

BEHIND THE SCENES

Quark was involved in Vantaka's scheme. The wily Ferengi assumed that the deal was off when Vantaka died. He was surprised to see a shadowy figure with Vantaka's voice insist that the deal was still on.

Dax studied Vantaka's effects and found he'd been working on a way to transfer consciousness from one body to another. Dax and the Doctor agreed that Vantaka's pursuer Kajada was the most likely suspect.

Odo excluded Kajada from the investigation, but it was really Dr. Bashir who had been taken over by Vantaka. The affair tested Odo and the crew of Deep Space Nine.

Odo found Lieutenant Primmin to be an asset in the investigation. He reconsidered his original harsh judgment of the young officer.

An alien named Croden was involved in a robbery planned by Quark. He killed a Miradorn in the process.

In custody, Croden was in danger of being killed by the Miradorn's surviving twin. Odo prevented vigilante justice from claiming his prisoner's life.

Croden had something of interest to Odo. He claimed to have visited a planet in the Gamma Quadrant where an entire civilization of shape shifters lived. He showed Odo an artifact containing a mineral that transformed into metal, then back again, right before his eyes.

Croden tried to win the shape shifting constable's sympathies with the alluring answer to the riddle of Odo's origins. He claimed to know the way to the shape shifter colony on an asteroid in the Chamra Vortex.

They discovered that Croden was wanted on several charges on his home world of Rakhar. He was considered to be an "enemy of the people."

Commander Sisko assigned Odo to return the prisoner to Rakhar. The voyage was complicated by the Miradorn. The Miradorn attacked as the runabout arrived near the Chamra Vortex. The Miradorn ship outclassed Odo's runabout so Odo entered the Vortex. The ionized gases hid them.

THE FUTURE
They landed on the asteroid of the shape shifters. Odo soon realized it was a ruse.

Croden's daughter is hidden in a cave, in a stasis device. She is the only survivor of Croden's family. The repressive government of his world killed his wives as punishment for his political opposition.

When the Miradorn attacked, they moved the girl to the runabout. They eluded the Miradorn who was destroyed when gasses surrounding his ship exploded.

ODO

Convinced Croden is driven to desperate measures by cruel injustice on his home world, Odo reported the man was killed on the asteroid. He then found Croden and his daughter passage on a Vulcan ship.

In gratitude, they give him the shape shifting pendant. Perhaps it will someday serve as a clue to his background.

Again Odo was motivated by justice. When he realized Croden was a victim of institutionalized injustice, he was willing to lie to help the man and his daughter.

Odo was once trapped in a turbolift with Lwaxana Troi. He captured the thief who stole Lwaxana's prized jewelry.

The notorious Betazoid woman became fascinated with Odo. She gave him more attention than he liked.

Systems failures on the space station trapped the two together. It was revealed Odo was raised in a lab on Bajor. He was used as a source of amusement and asked to change into many objects.

Odo's confessions were interrupted when the end of his daily cycle grew near. He had to revert to his liquid state. No one had ever seen him in that state before. He was embarrassed by its approach.

To put him at ease, Lwaxana Troi removed her bright red wig, revealing the more ordinary hair beneath. She then formed her skirt into a pouch to hide Odo. This scene was an interesting encounter in lowered defenses.

Later Lwaxana Troi hinted to Odo that their next encounter might be sexual. He had never met anyone like her and finds her intriguing.

ORIGINS Odo believed the answer to the riddle of his existence waited in the Gamma Quadrant. This was finally proven true. Odo encountered the race that spawned him on an unidentified planet. He learned they are the mysterious Founders, the rulers of The Dominion.

ODO

They joined in a ritual called "The Link" in which Odo learned what it means to be part of his people. Odo found his own sense of justice more developed than that of the Founders.

Odo now believes he has more in common with humans than his own people. He has chosen to stay with those he calls his friends.

Odo left the Founders to return to the Alpha Quadrant, although he believes he may one day return to experience the Link and teach the Dominion about justice.

QUARK

Quark is a Ferengi. By definition, he is a sly fox, willing to sell out his best friend for gold-pressed latinum. Yet the proprietor of the gambling establishment on the Promenade at Deep Space Nine is surprisingly complex. Sometimes, he is a hero; all too often, he is a villain. At times he is an irredeemably sexist pig, drooling over Dax and flirting shamelessly with Kira.

Quark ran his establishment for five years during the Cardassian occupation. He made great profits in the black market. He was preparing to leave due to the instability of the provisional government on Bajor when the Federation stepped in.

Trying for a final big haul, Quark sent his nephew Nog and a B'kaazi named Jas-qal to clean out the ore samples in Section A-14. When Nog was apprehended in the act, Sisko persuaded Quark to stay on the station. He made Quark a community leader, the bait to convince other merchants to remain.

Quark likes Bajorans because they leave him alone. He complains they make dreadful ale, insisting he never trusts ale from a God-fearing people.

Quark preferred working for the brutal and deceitful Cardassians. He took advantage of their vices, profiting from Cardassians seeking escape from the harrowing duties of an occupying army.

Bajorans often sought escape in a holosuite. Widows and orphans in refugee camps used imagination to forget the harsh realities of their existence. Quark was always made a dream come true in exchange for gold-pressed latinum.

THE SKILLED OPPORTUNIST
Quark is a wheeler and a dealer. He might be small potatoes compared to the hotshots and big ears in the Grand Nagus' entourage, but he has everything a Ferengi needs to make a killing in the

QUARK

cutthroat world of galactic commerce: an eye for opportunity, a talent for behind-the-scenes intrigue, and plenty of that ultimate Ferengi virtue, greed.

Quark believes himself more than simply a bartender. His establishment on the Promenade is more than a bar or a gambling den; it is the place to be in that sector of the galaxy, a magnet for business opportunities both legitimate and otherwise.

Quark is the unproclaimed king of Deep Space Nine's bustling Promenade. He has a hand in everyone's business. Constable Odo is often forced to turn to Quark for information.

Quark's business interests are varied. He uses his bar to meet aliens and humans who pass through the station, providing grist for his greed mill.

The gambling houses specializing in Dabo and other games of chance are often rigged by Quark. The upstairs holosuites cater to all fantasies. Quark always installs the latest erotic holo programs. A Ferengi is as sensuous as he is avaricious.

GRACE UNDER FIRE
Quark is well-versed in Ferengi politics. When Zek, the Grand Nagus of all Ferengi, retired, he named Quark to take control of the Ferengi Alliance.

Zek used Quark to get his son to show initiative. The son joined forces with Quark's brother, Rom, and attempted to assassinate Quark. When Odo saved Quark, the Ferengi demonstrated what humans would consider an unusual response: instead of being furious with Rom, he embraced his brother for his ambition.

Quark has saved the station and several key crew members. He has also helped invaders take over the station and hired assassins. His best moments came when he took command at Ops during an aphasia attack.

QUARK

Another high point for Quark came when the Ferengi accepted Odo's offer to become his deputy. Quark discovered the secret location of the "Circle's" headquarters.

The Bajoran revolutionary army, led by Minister Jaro Esso with support from fundamentalist Vedek Winn, planned to torture and kill Major Kira. Quark's crucial information allowed Sisko and Bashir to free her. Quark also saved Bajor from the Cardassians, who were secretly funding the attempt to overthrow the weakened provisional government.

Quark's low points include hiring mercenaries to take over a cargo ship. He even led them to the runabout.

BREAKING THE RULES
Quark helped another group of mercenaries, led by a renegade Trill, capture Deep Space Nine. The space station was running with a skeleton crew due to a massive plasma storm.

The Trill stole Dax, the symbiont, from the body of Jadzia, the host. This could have led to Jadzia's death, accept Sisko shot the renegade host. Dax returned to Jadzia. Quark felt guilty he caused Jadzia pain and so led the crew to regain control of the station.

Quark likes Dax. Ferengi live for fantasies. Quark and Dax often play card games.

Quark enjoyed a bizarre romance with an ambitious Ferengi. Quark was overcome with confusion when a new assistant, Pel, suddenly kissed him. Quark was relieved to discover that although passing for a man, his assistant was female. His relief lasted only until he passed out after realizing he had broken every Ferengi law by doing business with a female.

He was saved because the Grand Nagus was also doing business with her. Prosecuting Quark would have forced action against the Nagus.

CONSEQUENCES   Quark admired the woman but was too caught up in Ferengi beliefs to picture her clothed and involved in business. Ferengi women are kept nude, pregnant and ignorant; otherwise they would beat the socks off Ferengi men.

Quark now interacts with females of all species. A sexy Boslic freighter captain, for example, provided him with the key earring needed to rescue a Bajoran hero. He even negotiated with the unpleasant Klingon sisters, Lursa and B'Etor.

The wily Ferengi tries to be open-minded. Quark and Kira enjoy an unusual friendship. The key to understanding Quark is his relationship with his best friend and nemesis, Odo.

Quark performs occasional good deeds when they result in profit. He has a different moral code than the others. He sees nothing wrong with theft, accept the risk of getting caught. He was outraged when a former colleague robbed and killed a man during a business deal.

Sisko allows Quark to do business, refusing to enforce Starfleet regulations as long as Quark remains honest and acts within Bajoran rules and regulations.

Sisko's opinion of Quark is note clear. While Sisko finds him amusing, he has made it obvious to the Ferengi that he can close down his business at any time. Quark is wary of crossing Sisko.

ODO CONNECTION   Quark was the first regular to locate on the Promenade. He had met Kira Nerys the night before he met Odo. The Prefect of Bajor, Gul Dukat, appointed Odo to investigate the murder of a Bajoran who collaborated with the Cardassians.

Odo visited Quark to check Kira's alibi. At first Quark supported Kira's story. Then, when Odo threatened to charge Quark as an accomplice to the murder, he admitted she paid for the alibi.

Odo and Quark refuse to admit they are becoming friends of a sort. When Odo was suspected of murder, Quark rushed to the shape shifter's defense. He told the Bajoran bigots that Odo was neither a killer nor a collaborator.

After five years together on Deep Space Nine, Odo knows Quark can be nefarious. Odo often confronts Quark and accuses him of a specific crime. He usually has enough proof to implicate the Ferengi.

Quark then directs Odo to someone guiltier than he. That doesn't mean the Ferengi is innocent, but only a little bit guilty.

Odo and Quark maintain a truce. The security officer frequently needles Quark, particularly when Quark is the victim of someone else's shenanigans.

Odo has saved Quark's life. In "The Nagus," the Ferengi was targeted for assassination. Without the security chief's timely intervention, Quark would have been blasted out of an airlock.

The two engage in playful sparring. Quark often demands payment for his help and constantly reminds Odo of his duties. Odo makes it clear that he will not mourn Quark's passing. He suggests he will happily partake in the Ferengi tradition of buying and selling a piece of the corpse.

THE DEVIOUS   Quark can usually be found behind his bar. His brother Rom works for him in the bar, but Quark doesn't trust his fellow Ferengi.

Rom is devious but not very bright. He will always be under his brother's thumb. Quark and Rom are not equal partners in the gambling establishment on the Promenade.

Rom has tried to kill Quark, first with explosives, then by joining forces with the son of the Grand Nagus. He sent Quark out of an airlock without a pressure suit. Quark was proud of his brother for showing initiative.

Quark recently reassessed Rom's intelligence. He had always assumed Rom is an idiot. Then his brother showed he could work an electronic lock pick and use chemicals to burn into a safe. Rom showed remarkable skill, yet dubious judgment.

Odo is not so naive. He told Rom, "You're not as stupid as you look." Rom replied, "I am so!"

MAJOR KIRA
Kira holds little love for the "little troll," as she calls him. The two have been forced to work together. Kira endures Quark's incessant flirting and cannot understand how Dax can be friends with the Ferengi. Quark earned points with Kira when he brought her the earring of Li Nalas. Quark saved Kira's life when he discovered the secret hiding place of "The Circle."

Vedek Bareil admitted Quark is a friend. Kira was outraged when Quark allowed a renegade Trill and his Klingon accomplices to take control of Deep Space Nine.

A Ferengi, Quark is incurably sexist. He revels in making advances towards Major Kira. When she violently rebuffs him, he becomes more excited. When he put his hand on her waist, she threw him against a wall. He happily responded, "I love a woman in uniform!"

DAX, OBRIEN AND BASHIR
Quark loves Jadzia Dax, the lovely Trill whom he often serves Roctageno and spice pudding. Quark felt victimized when his attempt to fence stolen jewels led to Dax being removed from Jadzia. He didn't know the mercenaries would steal the symbiont. He started the rescue attempt.

Quark provides a sympathetic ear to Miles O'Brien. Miles is amused at Quark's antics. Quark encouraged O'Brien to risk his life and violate the Prime Directive to help Tosk.

Quark finds the libidinous Doctor Bashir amusing. Dr. Bashir treated Quark after members of the "Circle" branded their logo on Quark's head. Later, Quark was nearly killed when he was shot in the chest with a Compressed Tetryon beam.

Quark had found a list of Bajoran collaborators for the widow of the man whose murder first brought Odo to Deep Space Nine. Quark survived his injuries and a subsequent assassination attempt in sickbay. He eventually identified his attacker.

Quark is not a newcomer to Deep Space Nine. Quark ran his operations under the Cardassians. He bribed officials to look the other way.

The Cardassians appreciated the services offered by Quark's Place, particularly the range of sex in the holosuites. Nothing is too kinky for Quark so long as it's profitable. Cardassians respect Ferengi but don't trust them.

DEAL MAKER

Quark exhibits a range of emotions. When a former business partner was sent to a Romulan prison camp when a deal went sour, the Ferengi showed fear and cunning. He attempted to bribe his way off the man's death list. The criminal chose to commit more crimes rather than accept Quark's generous bribes. The crimes led to the thief's undoing.

Sisko has as little to do with Quark as possible. He kept Quark from closing his place and fleeing the station after the Cardassians left. Sisko knew that if Quark stayed, the other merchants would stay as well.

Quark justified remaining on Deep Space Nine by saying that the Federation would bring new business. The Ferengi didn't anticipate that the only stable wormhole in the galaxy would be discovered nearby. The space station became a key stopover point for commerce with the Gamma Quadrant.

Bajor was no longer a remote outpost. It became a major hub of the galaxy. New visitors arrive at the station daily. Quark's reluctant decision to remain became the best business decision in his life.

INSIDER TRADING Quark deals in information. He uses it to remain in Sisko's good graces. Although Sisko doesn't trust Quark, the senior staff knows what to expect from the Ferengi. They do not expect Quark to become honest overnight.

Odo makes sure Quark is aware of the penalties associated with a serious violation. When Quark is caught cheating he is forced to make restitution. Getting around rules and not being caught is one of the first skills a Ferengi learns.

"Quark's Place" is the main entertainment concession on the space station. Visitors head for Quark's establishment between trading trips. They find gambling and holosuites.

Originally the holosuites were brothels. Under pressure from Commander Sisko, they were reprogrammed for family entertainment.

ANGLES Quark is capable of good and bad. In "The Passenger" he supplied mercenaries to a serial killer. Willingly dealing with a murderer showed a disturbing side of Quark.

Quark lets others do time for his crimes. When he and a cousin sold defective warp engines to aliens, Quark implicated his cousin. The cousin went to prison instead of Quark.

When Quark engineered the hijacking of Romulan ale, he eluded conviction while his henchman earned eight years in a Romulan prison camp. Another cousin stole rare items from a museum and was caught sneaking aboard the space station to meet Quark. Although the Ferengi denied involvement, Quark was crestfallen to hear of his cousin's capture.

When Quark discovered that his new partner, Pel, was a female Ferengi disguised as a male, he relinquished all interest in a deal that was worth millions. He protected her and gained her free passage to the Gamma Quadrant.

Clearly Quark did not want to see her hurt. This showed a compassionate side to the Ferengi.

CHARMING FERENGI?

Quark is a charming representative of his species. "My benevolence is known throughout the galaxy," he crows at one point. One wonders what truth lies behind that grandiose boast. Perhaps this strangely repulsive charm makes Commander Benjamin Sisko tolerant of Quark.

Occasionally Quark helps solve a crisis. For example, he shut down his casino to fool Cardassians in "The Emissary." Quark knows how to get along with those in power.

Quark is a coward, although he once attacked a Klingon in "Invasive Procedures." Quark pretended to be injured and was taken to Sickbay so he could team up with Doctor Bashir. Together they overcame one of the desperadoes who had taken over the largely abandoned station.

Attacking a Klingon, even ineptly, takes courage. There may be a conscience between those huge lobes after all. In "Move Along Home," he is caught cheating at Dabo by visiting Wadi, the first aliens to officially come across from the Gamma Quadrant. He is forced to play their game known as Chula. Slowly, Quark begins to suspect the four game pieces he is moving represent Commander Sisko, Doctor Bashir, Major Kira and Dax.

Their lives hinge on the outcome of the game. Quark adjusts his playing to optimize their survival. They were never in real danger, but Quark didn't know that and swears he will never cheat again.

BUSINESS

Sometimes Quark lives dangerously. He sets up criminal activities, mostly thefts and robberies, through his vast information network. Even Odo admires the intelligence system.

When a robbery planned by Quark results in the death of a twinned Miradorn raider, Quark and Rom scramble to keep this information under

QUARK

wraps. The surviving Miradorn is bent on revenge and will kill them both if he learns of their involvement. Luckily the Miradorn is killed pursuing Odo, leaving the Ferengi brothers in the clear.

For a Ferengi, life is business. Quark seeks out new opportunities for profit from the comfortable hub of his thriving establishment. His head spins with dreams of gold-press latinum for his coffers.

With both feet firmly planted on the ground, he pursues his single-minded goal with great practicality. He is distracted only by the ongoing feud with the dour Odo. It would be hard to imagine Deep Space Nine without him.

COMMANDER BEN SISKO

After arriving on the space station Deep Space Nine, Commander Benjamin Sisko became more rested and relaxed. Sisko put the death of his wife, Jennifer, behind him.

She was killed three years earlier aboard the USS Saratoga. The vessel was attacked by the Borg near the M5 Red Dwarf star known as Wolf 359. The Borg ship encountered an armada of 40 Federation starships, including Klingon ships, and destroyed them all, resulting in almost ten thousand dead.

Ben Sisko, then First Officer of the Saratoga, and his son, Jake, were among the few survivors. The massacre, known as the Battle of Wolf 359, occurred on Stardate 43997.

Lt. Commander Sisko and his then nine-year-old son, Jake, made it into the Saratoga's escape pod just in time. Jennifer was killed by a crashing tritanium bulkhead.

Sisko refused to address his feelings in the aftermath of the battle. He used his late Vulcan captain as an example and buried the white-hot emotions. Memories of the Saratoga haunted every waking and sleeping moment.

The Bolian pulled his body to safety but left his mind and his soul behind, reeling from the screams of the dying as he watched the only thing that made his life worth living vanish. A black hole opened in his heart and sucked away his will until nothing mattered. Nothing except that one gift his wife had left him, the child who looked more and more like his mother each day. Ben wrestled with many demons before he and Jake could lead a normal life.

Starfleet believed Ben had let his career languish working in the Martian shipyards. Starfleet ordered him to take command of the former Cardassian space station in orbit around Bajor. The world was recently abandoned by ruthless Cardassian overlords.

TEARS
Sisko accepted the assignment to Deep Space Nine under protest. Ben and Jake arrived at Deep Space Nine on Stardate 46379.1. He was ready to bolt when he saw the crumbling station. He applied for a job as a professor at a Terran university and seriously considered leaving Starfleet to raise Jake on Earth.

Ben's life changed forever when he visited the Bajoran spiritual leader, Kai Opaka. She entrusted him with an "orb," known as the "Tear of the Prophet." The orb enabled him to relive the first time he met his late wife. To him it was not a vision, but very real.

The orb led Sisko and Dax to the stable wormhole connecting the Alpha Quadrant with the Gamma Quadrant. It lies some 70,000 light years away, 420 trillion miles from the farthest outpost in the Federation.

Sisko encountered the beings who constructed the orbs and built the wormhole. The Bajorans worship these beings as "Prophets of the Celestial Temple."

As he learned what people represent to the beings, he realized what he was missing. He relived the horror of the firestorm on the Saratoga and finally realized that his heart had never left the side of wife's body.

He saw her silent face in his dreams and in his waking hours. In the blink an eye he was back aboard the burning starship, his hand on hot metal, ready to give his life to restore life to the person who meant more to him than life itself.

Only his love for his son allowed Sisko to get to the escape pod. When Jake awoke in his hospital room and learned of his mother's death, the boy noticed a sad, almost sedate manner in his father. This continued until Ben was reborn in his visit to the wormhole. Ben had let a part of him die.

Seeing Jennifer again allowed him to grieve and finally reach acceptance. He forgave Picard, became a better father to Jake and learned to love life again.

JOURNEY

Sisko gained a new lease on life. He had developed an almost maddeningly detached command style after an incident in his first year at Starfleet Academy. An unannounced drill had caught him by surprise and he panicked. He learned to deal with crisis by keeping calm.

This trait encouraged unsuspecting adversaries to underrate him. His calm demeanor hid a quick mind. Enterprise Captain Picard is cool under fire, but Sisko withdraws into a calm that affects those around him, especially junior officers under his command.

The Saratoga's late captain, a Vulcan named Storil, profoundly influenced Sisko's life. Ben marveled at the calm way the Vulcan gave his last orders. He affected a similar calm when forced to take command of the ship and organize the evacuation of civilians and surviving crew.

He then went to find Jennifer and Jake in their quarters. The journey did not end with the rescue of his son and the death of his wife. It only ended after Sisko's fulfillment of the Bajoran prophecy that a non-believer would find the temple and save the prophets from attack.

Sisko shook off the accolades that accompany his position as "Emissary" in the Bajoran religion. He is extremely annoyed by the constant need to let Bajoran Kai and Vedeks read his "pagh," or life-force, each time they encounter him.

Sisko noted the parallel between his attempt to rebuild his life and Bajor's efforts to repair the damage caused by the Cardassians. He learned to relate to his new crew after his transformation in the wormhole.

TALENTS

Sisko is an amateur astronomer. He studies Bajoran constellations. His favorite is "The Runners." Sisko wondered whether they were running toward or away from something.

He is a skilled chef, a trait learned from his father. He was especially fond of his father's aubergine stew, a dish that he often makes for Jake and Dax.

Sisko is a poet at heart. He loves baseball and has spent hours on holodecks recreating games. He speaks with great reverence for a game that ceased to exist centuries before he was born. Sisko even developed relationships with some of the players, which proved useful when an alien being took the form of Harmon "Buck" Bukai, the shortstop, third baseman for the London Kings who broke Joe Dimaggio's 56 game hitting streak in 2026.

Sisko stands up for his people. He publicly defended Odo and Dax when each was charged with murder. Sisko and Kira often butt heads over Bajoran and Starfleet interests differ, but the two enjoy a working relationship based on mutual respect and function as a team.

FIRM Sisko gained the respect of Bajoran and Federation alike with his calm, measured responses to crisis and his attempts to balance Bajoran religion with the need to teach science.

Sisko has stood up to Vedek Winn, informing the Bajoran that he is neither devil nor enemy. Kira admitted Sisko is not a devil, bringing a rare smile to Sisko's face.

Sisko is learning to deal with Jake's growing up. He is concerned about his son's friendship with Nog. He is also insulted that Nog's father, Rom, is equally concerned about Jake's influence on Nog.

Jake has a girlfriend, a Dabo girl who works for Quark. Ben has more trouble accepting this than accepting that Jake does not want to join Starfleet when he comes of age.

Ben is a good father. He required Jake to study Klingon opera, as he had been when he was young. Jake asked his father why he should study something so useless. Ben fumbled for an answer, suggesting Jake might work with Klingons.

Sisko's interpersonal abilities showed well in the case of a terraformer who lost his life in the creation of a new star. Ben found himself in an uncomfortable position. He admired the egotistical planet maker and was unnerved to discover that the beautiful young woman he loved was married to the older scientist.

She was an empathic projection telepath and would fall into a coma while her subconscious projected an image of herself. The unconscious image fell in love with Ben. Although the woman is cold to Ben and remembers nothing, her telepathic image remembers everything but is banished when the woman wakes.

POETRY

The proud, defiant scientist gives his life to spare her the continued pain of life-long mating to an egotist, the pain that drove her into the coma. As he died, the wild scientist sparked an emotion in Sisko by mentioning an old Klingon poem.

Sisko understood the reference. The terraformer died in response to the "Tale of Kang." The poem vividly described how great it is to die at the peak of one's existence. It tells how magnificent it is to pass this veil beloved, never to have been seen in tragic decline.

The tragic Shakespearean lilt of Kang led him to perceive there would be nothing worse than being an ancient warrior, pitied because he had slain all of his enemies, with no more worlds to conquer. The scientist refused to be pitied, finishing a magnificent stellar first-time-ever event, the artificial creation of a star, to end his career on a perfect high note.

Ben recognized the poem. When the duty officer did not understand the suicidal planet maker's ramblings, Sisko quietly said, "Klingon poetry." He promised to deliver the scientist's obituary to the Daystrom Institute. An egotist to the end, the planet maker had written it himself.

The unifying factor among the bridge crew has been the appearance of the "Q" entity. It arrived with Vash, a Terran archeologist, and former lover of

Jean-Luc Picard, who was brought back from the Gamma Quad-rant by a runabout. Vash had preceded Ben and Jadzia into the Gamma Quadrant accepting an offer from Q. The entire crew of Deep Space Nine united in their hatred of Q.

SISKO AND DAX

Benjamin Sisko first met Curzon Dax, who served as his mentor, years before. At that time Dax was a kindly old man.

Ben knew that Dax would join him on DS9. He was surprised, and amused, that Dax was now a beautiful young woman. Whenever Sisko sees Julian or another young man attempt seduction, he is reminded of the kindly old man, smiling with the same bemused expression as Jadzia.

Curzon Dax was once a hard-drinking, two-fisted fighter, a womanizer and borderline sexist. Now Dax has been both sexes and shares memories of a boy, a girl, a mother and a father. Dax has been all things. Sisko is still learning to adapt to the new being named Jadzia Dax.

Ben first met Jadzia when she and Julian reported for duty aboard Deep Space Nine. It was not long before Sisko defended his old friend from charges of treason, conspiracy and murder, acts which occurred when she was still Curzon Dax.

Dax was guilty only of adultery with the late General Tundro's widow, who finally confessed to give Dax an alibi. The widow's confession soiled her reputation but kept alive the legend of the general killed in an ambush after betraying his own troops.

Sisko often seeks out Dax's serene wisdom and sense of humor. She noted that Curzon appreciated Ben's baseball stories more than she does, but she enjoys Benjamin's company. Dax knows that, barring unseen accident, she will outlive Sisko and all her compatriots on Deep Space Nine.

Jadzia will eventually die but Dax will live on. Dax has buried numerous hosts, foes, children, families, friends and co-workers. Like Spock, Data and perhaps Odo, she must deal with the short lives of her friends. This is a special sadness reserved for the Trill.

SISKO AND KIRA

The relationship between Sisko and Kira is complex. The feisty Bajoran freedom fighter spent her life trying to free her people from a powerful empire, only to see her planet invite in another in the form of the Federation. When Sisko arrived, he evicted her from the prefect's office, which she had taken as her own after Gul Dukat fled. She also noted Sisko's hatred for Picard, whom he is unable to separate from his memories of Locutus of Borg, the leader of the Borg massacre at Wolf 359.

She was later surprised when Sisko pitched in to help her clean up. She began to re-evaluate him after he was summoned by the Kai and chosen as the "Emissary" to the prophets in the "Celestial Temple."

The events were similar to a dream shared by Kira and Sisko, about Kai Opaka and the orbs. Opaka is a central figure in Kira's life. Sisko's relationship with the Kai improved relations between Kira and Sisko.

Kira criticized Starfleet commanders when Sisko first arrived. He gained her respect by standing up to her and blackmailing Quark.

RELIGION

The complex Bajoran mix of religion and science led to heated exchanges between Kira and Sisko. For example, Major Kira initially backed Vedek Winn's attempt to intimidate Keiko into changing her school curriculum. After Winn bombed the school and the attempted assassination of Bareil, Ben got the Bajoran nationals to stand with the Deep Space Nine crew.

This support proved vital when "The Circle" began their conspiracy. For a time it cost Kira her job as First Officer and Deep Space Nine Liaison to Bajor. Eventually helped forge friendships between Kira and her crewmates. One by one, each came to her quarters to let her know how much she means to them.

Sisko stood up to Minister Jaro and complained about her removal. He vowed to Kira that he would get her back and mounted an armed rescue attempt to save her from fundamentalists. Fellow Bajorans were torturing her when Sisko, Bashir and the rescue party acted on "deputy" Quark's tip and arrived just in time to save her.

Major Kira joined Dax in exposing the conspiracy. The anti-Cardassian "Circle" actually planned to hand Bajor back to the Cardassians, who secretly provided weapons to the "Circle." The Cardassians wanted control of the wormhole.

Kira and Sisko share a dislike for Cardassians, yet each has done their duty and dealt in a civil fashion with Cardassians. Sisko and Kira share this character trait with Miles O'Brien.

Sisko took perverse pleasure forcing Julian to endure what he lived through in his youth. He made the doctor escort alien ambassadors and pointed out how Curzon Dax used to do the same to him. The young doctor's quick thinking saved the life of the Vulcan, Bolian and the female alien ambassador.

BASHIR, ODO AND QUARK

Sisko told Odo he likes him because he is blunt. He always knows where Odo stands. He also appreciates Odo's zeal for justice and security. Odo was not optimistic about having a Starfleet officer in command but he was impressed when Sisko blackmailed Quark. Sisko won Odo's respect when he gave him authority over Starfleet security operations.

Sisko used Ferengi psychology in his first encounter with Quark, and quickly gained the Ferengi's respect. Sisko plea bargained to force Quark's hand.

Quark expected words to win his nephew's freedom. Then Sisko blackmailed him. Sisko does not trust Quark; he knows how to interact, but always remembers he is dealing with a Ferengi.

MILES AND KEIKO

Sisko liked Miles O'Brien at first sight. He found the former Enterprise transporter chief to be a true miracle worker. Sisko and Miles have a close relationship. He appreciates his capable engineer, especially when the lives of every being on the station hang in the balance.

Sisko was pleased when Keiko volunteered to open a school on Deep Space Nine. He worried about Jake having to study alone. A school keeps the children on the station out of trouble. Ben provided computers and space. His sending Jake encouraged other parents to give the school a chance.

Sisko stood up for her when the fundamentalist Bajoran, Vedek Winn, attempted to shut the school. Some parents objected to the study of vertiron particles. Bajorans think this is blasphemy since the wormhole is regarded as the "Celestial Temple."

Sisko enlisted Vedek Bareil to fend off Winn. Sisko then saved Bareil from an assassin.

JAKE

The relationship between Ben and his son is very complex and tests the demands of duty. Father and son still deal with the death of Jennifer Sisko.

Sisko tries to be Jake's friend as well as his father. Ben feels that he neglected his son while blinded by grief for his wife. He also feels guilty about putting Jennifer and Jake at risk on the Saratoga. Ben's transformation in the wormhole helped restore the father Jake had lost.

The two enjoy baseball. Ben actively offers a role model and forces Jake to do homework and improve himself. He is not afraid to show feelings, kissing an embarrassed Jake on the forehead or hugging him on the Promenade. Jake is glad to have his dad back.

PICARD   When Sisko arrived at Deep Space Nine, he encountered Jean-Luc Picard. Sisko had once met him in battle, after Picard had been transformed into Locutus by the Borg. Sisko knew Picard was not to blame for his actions, but emotionally could not separate Picard from the being that killed Jennifer.

Picard had never met a survivor of Wolf 359. Sisko later realized he added to Picard's pain and regretted reopening the painful wound.

Later Ben accepted Jennifer's death. He withdrew his request for a transfer and realized Picard and himself shared grief. Ben finally understood Picard remembered the deaths and felt responsible,

Picard realized Ben lost his wife in the tragedy and vowed to help Ben and Jake, and thus ease his own heart. The two parted as friends as Ben Sisko put the events of Wolf 359 behind him.

THE ALIENS:
BAJORANS, CARDASSIANS AND FERENGI

by Trey Causey

STAR TREK—DEEP SPACE NINE uses many races, cultures and institutions originally presented on STAR TREK—THE NEXT GENERATION. Unlike the relationship between the original series and THE NEXT GENERATION, DEEP SPACE NINE occurs at the same time as the program that spawned it. The difference is its focus on a specific part of the galaxy. DEEP SPACE NINE centers on the Federation's relationship with the Cardassian union and the planet Bajor.

Both races first appeared in THE NEXT GENERATION. They were fleshed out in DEEP SPACE NINE and somewhat altered from their original conception.

The Ferengi, a recurring villain on THE NEXT GENERATION, entered the spotlight on DEEP SPACE NINE with a Ferengi-run bar on the station. DEEP SPACE NINE made all three alien races into realistic characters.

THE BAJORANS
The Bajorans inhabit a planet overrun by the Cardassians. They presented a moral dilemma to the Federation since their first appearance on the NEXT GENERATION episode, "Ensign Ro." The title character is a Bajoran Starfleet officer who served time in prison for insubordination resulting in the death of crew members.

Ro is freed in return for helping the Enterprise track down those responsible for an attack on a Federation colony, a Bajoran terrorist group. The attack came from Cardassians, but the dilemma still stands.

The, peaceful, spiritual Bajorans saw their homeworld raped by Cardassians. The Federation is not willing to wage war with the Cardassians. Bajoran terrorists are sometimes indiscriminate about targets.

DEEP SPACE NINE takes place against this backdrop. The freed Bajorans find themselves dependent on the Federation for protection. After suffering years of Cardassian rule, the Bajoran people have trouble governing themselves. These are not good times for Bajor.

DEEP SPACE NINE portrays the complex issues facing Bajor. The Bajorans are not always portrayed guiltless. In the episode "Past Prologue," a Bajoran terrorist tries to blow up the wormhole. Major Kira stops the attempt.

The episode "In The Hands of the Prophets" portrays a religious leader of Bajor opposed to the scientific beliefs taught Bajoran children in the school on Deep Space Nine. The leader also attempts to assassinate a rival. In the episode "Duet" a Bajoran kills a Cardassian simply because he is Cardassian.

Bajoran religion, only touched on in THE NEXT GENERATION, is revealed in detail in DEEP SPACE NINE. The Kai, the Bajoran equivalent of the Pope, appears in two episodes. Later, the politics of religion are glimpsed as the Vadek Assembly convenes to elect a new Kai.

Bajoran religion is portrayed in a positive light, but some individuals hold evil goals. The greatest threat to continued peace on Bajor may come from the Bajorans.

THE CARDASSIANS

Cardassians first appeared on an episode of THE NEXT GENERATION titled "The Wounded." That episode, and others that followed, showed the Cardassians as a warlike, highly militaristic people in tenuous peace with the Federation. The Cardassians appeared as adversaries in episodes of THE NEXT GENERATION. DEEP SPACE NINE gave them major villain status.

Deep Space Nine was a Cardassian mining facility during their occupation of Bajor. The station, then known as Terok Nor, was commanded by Gul Dukat. The Federation moved in after the Cardassians withdrew from the system in the episode "Emissary."

The strategic importance of the wormhole made the Cardassians eager to regain control of Bajor. The Cardassians hatched numerous plots during the first two seasons of DEEP SPACE NINE. All were thwarted by the crew of Deep Space Nine.

Several episodes, most notably "Duet," portrayed individual Cardassians in a positive light. Even Gul Dukat, the villain in several early episodes, developed into more of a character in the two part episode "The Maquis." He became almost sympathetic.

Though still enemies of the Federation, the Cardassians no longer appear relentlessly evil but more and more individual with complex and varied personalities. The last episode of DEEP SPACE NINE's second season to feature the Cardassians, "Tribunal," returned them to their villainous roots.

THE FERENGI

The Ferengi passed through several changes since their first appearance on the NEXT GENERATION episode "The Last Outpost." The mercantile Ferengi began as barbaric, animalistic, powerful foes of the Federation.

The premiere episode of TNG, "Encounter At Farpoint," never shows Ferengi. The dialogue implies they are a major power opposing the Federation, and possibly cannibalistic!

The portrayal of Ferengi softens after this. Though they appear villainous in many more NEXT GENERATION episodes, the race ceases to be a major threat to the Federation, but more an intergalactic nuisance. Ferengi are played for comedy relief much of the time, and act like goblins or trolls out of juvenile fantasy literature rather than as members of a vast outer space empire.

DEEP SPACE NINE brought new, recurring Ferengi characters, Quark, the successful businessman, and his bumbling brother, Rom and Rom's son, Nog. The Ferengi on DEEP SPACE NINE reinforce the comedic role notably in "The Nagus."

The Ferengi remain intensely greedy beings, but a lecherous streak has been added. No episode of the new series has portrayed Ferengi as villains, although some of Quark's freewheeling business deals strays close to edge, such as dealing with a serial killer in "The Passenger."

DEEP SPACE NINE continues the comedic portrayal of Ferengi while it reveals their society and culture. A Ferengi woman was seen for the first time in the episode "Rules of Acquisition." The titular rules are quoted by Quark and others throughout the first two seasons.

The Ferengi ruler, The Nagus, appeared in two episodes of DEEP SPACE NINE, "The Nagus" and "Rules of Acquisition." More is learned about the Ferengi each time he turns up.

DEEP SPACE NINE presents sympathetic Ferengi for the first time. Quark, for all his criminal scheming, is part of Deep Space Nine. His relationship with Odo, his dogged adversary and only friend, is an interesting aspect of the series. Quark may develop further as an important member of the crew.

The season two finale, "The Jem 'Hedar," includes a sequence when Quark engages Commander Sisko in spirited debate over Federation prejudice against Ferengi. He asks Sisko if he would object to his son marrying a Ferengi woman. Sisko replies that he's never thought about it. Quark states this is his point.

Quark defends his Ferengi heritage by pointing out that they never engaged in wars pitting one nation against another such as on Earth. Ferengi did appear warlike in "The Last Outpost" and "The Battle," so there is more than Quark admits. Quark always admits only what he has to.

None of the principal alien societies were introduced on DEEP SPACE NINE. All began on STAR TREK—THE NEXT GENERATION, then were more fully developed on this series. The final episode of the second season introduces a fourth major alien race, The Dominion. This new addition may have profound effects on the other races which people DEEP SPACE NINE.

THE DOMINION

Episode seven, "Rules of Acquisition," and episode ten, "Sanctuary," early in the second season of DEEP SPACE NINE, reveal the existence of a mysterious alien race called The Dominion. In "Rules of Acquisition" aliens in the Gamma Quadrant say no significant trade agreements are made without the approval of the Dominion. The alien making the statement clearly believes that not getting this approval would be a grave mistake.

In "Sanctuary" three million refugees pour through the wormhole escaping from a world in bondage. They escaped after the Dominion conquered their slave masters. The identity and nature of the Dominion are not revealed.

Hints clearly foreshadowed appearance by the Dominion. Nothing could have prepared viewers for what followed.

"Rules of Acquisition" shows that the Dominion control major trade agreements in the Gamma Quadrant. That still doesn't reveal much about them. They could be a powerful mercantile cartel controlling economic life in the Gamma Quadrant or a more organized version of the Ferengi.

Zek, the Grand Nagus, knew the importance of the Dominion, but failed trying to contact them. Clearly they will be found only when they want to be found.

WAITING
Reference to the Dominion in "Sanctuary" proved they were powerful. They had conquered a race that enslaved three million people.

Allowing three million refugees to escape showed the Dominion had no interest in being slave masters. At the time it seemed the Dominion might be a powerful but benevolent race.

THE DOMINION

It is also possible the Dominion had no use for former slaves and were uncaring of their fate. They may have known that a fleet of refugees would discover the wormhole and bring the news to the rest of the Scrians.

What happened next tested Federation policies when confronted by three million refugees. The Federation found them a planet even after Bajor refused them.

The Dominion proved to be much more than expected in the second season finale, "The Jem 'Hedar." Commander Sisko and Quark are imprisoned inside a force field while visiting a planet in the Gamma Quadrant. The holding cells kill when touched.

Quark and Sisko share their cell with a telepath fugitive. The telepath turns out to be a spy "rescued" along with Sisko and Quark and returned to the space station. She expects to find a niche in the Federation to spy on them. Quark exposes her so she vanishes via transporter technology unknown to the Federation.

WATCHING

A year and a half passed before the Dominion blockaded the wormhole, forbidding entry to the Federation. They observed the Federation during that time. The Dominion may be conquerors or they may believe the Federation will not tolerate their heavy handed methods. It is also not clear if the Dominion is monolithic.

Eris failed to use her imprisonment with Sisko and Quark to learn more about the Federation and its representatives. The Dominion may possess mistaken notions about the Federation or not be aware Starfleet operates with a code of non-interference under the Prime Directive. The Klingons at the time of James T. Kirk had no such code. The Dominion also may not. According to the episode, "Sanctuary," the Dominion invaded and conquered a planet.

The Dominion may occupy the position formerly held by the Klingons in 23rd century STAR TREK. They effectively declared war on the Federation.

Every future DEEP SPACE NINE episode must reflect that threat that lies just beyond the wormhole.

THREATENING

This threat cannot be ignored. The Jem 'Hedar, the enforcers of the Dominion, admitted participating in the destruction of New Bajor, the Bajoran colony recently established in the Gamma Quadrant. Major Kira wants revenge.

The battle in which the USS Odyssey was destroyed was the first step in a war. The vessel had been on a mission to rescue Commander Sisko and Quark and retreated as soon as he was retrieved. The Dominion destroyed the Odyssey while it was in retreat.

The destruction of New Bajor emerges as a rallying cry for all Bajorans. Kai Winn must deal with this. She dislikes the Federation, but Bajor lacks firepower. The Cardassian occupation is too fresh in the minds of Bajorans for them to ignore this blatant attack by the Dominion. Bajor is not far from the wormhole. It needs the protection of the Federation against the powerful forces of the Dominion.

The Dominion may not attack Bajor, but by forbidding the Federation access to the wormhole, they create confrontation. Deep Space Nine must become the center for Federation military response through the wormhole.

WHO ARE THE MAQUIS?

History chronicles the tale of rebels fighting against oppression many times in many places, whether American colonists against England in the 18th Century or Federation colonists against the Cardassians in the 24th Century.

The treaty ending the war between Cardassia Prime and the Federation allows both Cardassian and Federation colonists to live side by side in the Cardassian Demilitarized zone. The colonists live in separate cities with each side sacrificing land, but distrust and resentment linger.

Federation colonists remember Cardassian war crimes, although they were never victims. Some colonists gave up farms they'd worked for years.

Cardassians distrust Federation colonists so Central Command supplies weapons for defense. This is not widely known on Cardassia because Zeppelites act as intermediaries to hide shipments from Federation scrutiny.

BORDER WAR
Incidents gradually escalate into open warfare. Colonists are convinced Cardassians smuggle weapons. They sabotaged one gun-running ship, killing 70 Cardassians. The sabotage took place at Deep Space Nine.

When a Federation merchant ship refused to allow Cardassians to board for investigation on the frontier it was fired on by two Cardassian shuttles. A heavily armed Federation vessel responded to the merchant ship's distress call and destroyed the Cardassian attackers. This led to a war of words never adequately settled.

Gul Dukat didn't believe Cardassians supplied arms until the Central Command tried to frame *him* for it. An outraged Dukat personally halted the arms shipments enforcing the Cardassian/Federation treaty, much to the chagrin of the Cardassian Central Command.

THE MAQUIS

Despite this progress, the rebel Federation colonists, the Maquis, attacked an arms depot in a Cardassian frontier colony, forcing a confrontation with Ben Sisko. Former Starfleet officer Calvin Hudson was piloting one of the shuttles for the Maquis. They called off their attack but clearly stated they will settle for nothing less than abandonment of the frontier worlds by the Cardassians.

CARDASSIAN CRIMES
The two part DEEP SPACE NINE story that introduced the Maquis tells of Cardassian attacks on civilians but none are shown. A member of the Maquis is captured and interrogated by the Cardassians. He confesses. Afterwards he supposedly commits suicide in his cell. The suspicious death angers the Maquis.

Halting Cardassian arms smuggling increases their desperation. Cardassians believe the Federation secretly arms their colonists but have been unable to discover an official connection between the Federation and the Maquis. Starfleet officially hunts the Maquis and declares them criminals. This frustrates Cardassian attempts even more but they still believe the Federation culpable.

The Cardassians manufacture evidence. In the DEEP SPACE NINE episode "Tribunal," the Cardassians kidnap Miles O'Brien from his shuttle and take him to Cardassia Prime. He is subjected to humiliating treatment by the Cardassians.

They insist he confess to crimes. When he asks what he's charged with, he is told it doesn't matter because he has already been found guilty. The advocate appointed by the Cardassians to defend him at trial insists Miles confess for the good of all. His execution has already been scheduled.

Odo and Sisko unmask the real culprit, a Cardassian spy who replaced a human prisoner during the Cardassian/Federation conflict. The man was a shipmate of O'Brien under Captain Maxwell. O'Brien spoke with the man briefly on the space station before leaving with his wife for a vacation.

THE BATTLE

When Sisko arrives on Cardassia Prime with the spy, the prosecutors still find O'Brien guilty. They show mercy by releasing him to the Federation.

The Cardassian Central Command does not want the embarrassment of Sisko revealing their spy after convicting O'Brien of a crime he did not commit. The Cardassians know O'Brien is innocent but believe someone in the Federation is guilty. O'Brien is a scapegoat for trial.

The Cardassians are desperate to find an official link between the Federation and the Maquis. The Maquis have become a major threat. The barely organized group of farmers and former Starfleet officers have photon torpedoes and other advanced weapons.

Quark acted as intermediary for a huge arms shipment before he learned about the Maquis. The Vulcan woman he sold them to, Secona, provided the Maquis with the weapons for her own reasons. It is not clear why a Vulcan would side with rebels in the Demilitarized Zone.

The seventh season NEXT GENERATION episode "Preemptive Strike" features the return of Ro Laren. He had not been seen for two years.

The Enterprise is on its way to a rendezvous with Admiral Nachayev to discuss the Maquis and Cardassians in the Demilitarized Zone when "Preemptive Strike" opens. A welcome back party is being held for Ro Laren aboard the Enterprise. Ro was recently promoted to Lieutenant following her successful completion of the rigorous Advanced Tactical Training course. She is clearly uncomfortable with the attention so Picard has her summoned to the bridge. Actually he's waiting just outside the door of the reception room.

OUT-GUNNED

Jean-Luc congratulates Lieutenant Ro for her accomplishment. She thanks Captain Picard for recommending her for the program.

THE MAQUIS

The Enterprise responds to a distress call from a Cardassian vessel in the Demilitarized Zone as Picard and Ro go to the bridge. Long range sensors show a Cardassian ship under attack from several small Federation ships.

The ships look like Maquis. The Enterprise warns the Maquis to call off their attack or face immediate reprisals. They ignore the warning.

The Enterprise detonates photo torpedoes to keep the Maquis ships from the Cardassians. The Maquis halt their attack and withdraw.

The Enterprise assists the Cardassian wounded. In the Enterprise sickbay Jean-Luc argues with Gul Evek over the handling of the Maquis. Picard points out that Cardassian colonists destroyed a vessel in the DMZ the week before. Gul Evek states that if the Federation cannot deal with the problem the Cardassian military will have no choice but to intervene.

SECRET AGENT
The Cardassian ship continues on its way and the Enterprise rendezvous with Admiral Nachayev. Captain Picard and the Admiral discuss the Maquis. The Federation fears that the Maquis are moving beyond self-defense into war.

The Admiral informs Picard that they want to infiltrate the Maquis. A new war with Cardassia could cause hundreds of thousands of deaths. Starfleet has chosen Lt. Ro Laren as their operative. Ro accepts to validate Captain Picard's faith in her.

Ro Laren enters a bar on a planet in the Cardassian Demilitarized Zone. She wears civilian garb.

Worf and Data follow and announce that they are looking for a Bajoran woman who killed a Cardassian soldier. No one appears upset.

Ro is hides in a culvert with another man. She kisses him so as not to be discovered. The barkeeper tells Worf he doesn't know where she went.

After Worf and Data leave, Ro thanks the barkeeper. He engages her in conversation. She explains that she doesn't like Cardassians and wants to meet others of like mind.

Suddenly the barkeeper stuns Ro. She wakes in a room with three Maquis.

They interrogate Ro. She reveals that she grew up in Bajoran refugee camps and saw her father slain by Cardassians as a child. She wants to join them when she learns they're Maquis.

FATHER FIGURE

An elderly Maquis, Macius, takes a special liking to her. He explains that the settlement he lived in was on the Cardassian side of the zone after the Treaty. They pulled him from his bed one night and beat him. The Federation only offered their regrets.

Macius reveals he once had a good Bajoran friend who made Haspirate far stronger than the food replicators produce. His friend died fighting against the Cardassians on Bajor. Ro reveals that her father made very strong Haspirate, and she remembers the recipe. She offers to make some for Macius.

Later, Ro Laren meets a Maquis council. They've heard that the Cardassians will supply their colonists with biogenic weapons. The Maquis want to prevent this with a preemptive strike but they need more medical supplies.

It isn't explained how a preemptive strike would discourage the Cardassians from supplying their colonists with weapons. The Cardassians have always responded to force in kind.

Ro agrees to help the Maquis secure medical supplies. She says she can steal some from the Enterprise.

The Maquis council hesitate because they know little about Ro even though her imprisonment and release by Starfleet checks out. Macius trusts Ro and sways the council. One Maquis will accompany her.

THINGS PAST

A week has passed since Ro Laren left the Enterprise. The Enterprise receives a distress call from a vessel in the Topin System. When they respond, Ro sends the Enterprise a secret message.

Picard lets Ro's ship penetrate the aft shield to steal medical supplies. Ro succeeds only because Picard allows her to.

In the DMZ Macius and Ro become friends. She's given her own ship and allowed to go where she pleases.

Ro returns to the bar to report to Picard. He reveals that the Federation plans to entrap the Maquis.

In the DMZ Ro tells the Maquis that a Pakled ship carries components needed to make biogenic weapons. Ro and Macius philosophize about how long it will take to get the Cardassians to back down. Ro sees traits in Macius similar to those of her late father.

Ro tells Macius how her father comforted her as a child when she was frightened by "monsters under her bed." Her father played the Bajoran Clavion and told his daughter that the sound of the instrument would keep bad things away. Macius also plays the Clavion in memory of his departed Bajoran friend. This scene reveals more about Ro's past life.

CONSEQUENCES

Macius and Ro go to the marketplace to get the makings of a feast to "celebrate nothing." En route they see three mysterious robed Cardassians randomly firing on people.

Ro and Macius are given weapons. Macius is shot when he tries to help a wounded man. A furious Ro Laren shoots the Cardassian responsible.

She bends over Macius' body. The dying man tells her someone will take his place in the movement. Ro is overcome by grief. Macius had become a father figure to her. This is the second father she has seen killed by Cardassians.

This episode of THE NEXT GENERATION differs from the two part DEEP SPACE NINE episode that introduced the Maquis. It shows how life in the Federation colonies in the Cardassian Demilitarized Zone led to the birth of the Maquis.

The Maquis attack Cardassian weapons smugglers, but they do not execute civilians. This brutal side of Cardassian colonists justifies the Maquis' actions. The Maquis are clearly telling the truth when they say the Federation doesn't understand life in the colonies.

The two-part "The Maquis" took a neutral position showing faults on both sides. "Preemptive Strike" shows that Federation colonists were provoked into warfare.

TURNING POINT

Ro Laren's loyalties are challenged. She tries to persuade Jean-Luc to call off the mission. She even lies, saying the Maquis are unwilling to attack a convoy of six ships.

Picard recognizes something is wrong. Ro admits she's uncertain how she feels about the Maquis.

Jean-Luc says he will have Lt. Laren court marshaled if she sabotages the mission. She agrees to go on, but Captain Picard insists that Riker accompany her.

The Enterprise waits for the Maquis attack. The Maquis ships enter formation in the DMZ, but Ro warns the Maquis at the last moment. They retreat.

Ro pulls a gun on Will Riker. She explains that it's been a long time since she felt she belonged somewhere.

Will Riker understands, particularly when she expresses profound regret over letting down Captain Picard. She escapes to one of the Maquis ships. Will returns to the Enterprise.

Riker tells Picard that she honestly felt she was doing the right thing. Jean-Luc regrets failing to sway Ro Laren from the life-changing path she took.

WAR PATH

"Tribunal" showed desperate Cardassians battling the threat of the Maquis. They felt provoked by an intolerable situation.

"Preemptive Strike" presents a genuine turning point. The Cardassians commit crimes against unarmed civilians. Ro Laren relives her childhood nightmare and is changed by what she sees.

"Preemptive Strike" shows that war between the Federation and Cardassia is inevitable. Attacks on civilian colonists will swell the forces of the Maquis. Even members of Starfleet are quitting to enlist. Ro Laren remarks that one of her instructors at the school for Advanced Tactical Training resigned his commission to join the Federation colonists in the Demilitarized Zone.

Battle on this frontier will sweep the Federation and Cardassia back into the conflict they ended ten years before. Along with the threat of the Dominion and the Borg, the Federation now faces new war.

DEEP SPACE

The Stories

ARMAGEDDON GAME

Written by Morgan Gendel; Directed by Winrich Kolbe

Regular Cast:
Avery Brooks as Commander Benjamin Sisko; Rene Auberjonois as Odo; Siddig El Fadil as Doctor Bashir; Terry Farrell as Lieutenant Dax; Cirroc Lofton as Jake Sisko; Colm Meaney as Chief O'Brien; Armin Shimerman as Quark; Nana Visitor as Major Kira

Guest Stars:
Darleen Carr as Ambassador E'Tyshra; Rosalind Chao as Keiko O'Brien

This story casts Miles O'Brien and Dr. Julian Bashir into a life-or-death situation where this usually feuding pair must depend on each other to survive. Winrich Kolbe's directs the story. It begins with the two Deep Space Nine crew members working on an orbiting scientific platform above the planet T'Lani 3. A long-standing war between the T'Lani and the Kelleruns has recently ended.

Weapons known as "harvesters," engineered microbes that disrupt humanoid genetic material, remain stored on the station.

After a week Julian Bashir finds the correct frequency of muon radiation to neutralize the harvesters. The crisis is not immediately resolved. The job still remains undone with thousands of harvester samples yet to be destroyed.

Time passes. Kellerun raiders storm the lab when the last cylinder is about to be destroyed. O'Brien and Bashir overcome some raiders and gain weapons. The rest of the scientists are killed. The sound of weapons fire indicates killing continues in the rest of the station. O'Brien has been splashed with a few drops of the final harvesters sample.

They beam down to T'Lani 3, a planet devastated by the war. The ruins of a bombed-out building provides shelter.

Bashir wants to run. The battle-tested O'Brien says they must remain in one place. It will make it harder for the Kelleruns to find them.

Their hiding place has military rations and a non-functional transmitter. O'Brien sets to fixing it. Soon O'Brien falls ill, and Bashir discovers he's been infected by harvester microbes.

Kellerun and T'Lani ambassadors board Deep Space Nine and inform Commander Sisko that his two officers are dead. They lie, saying O'Brien triggered an old security program in the lab creating a radiation burst that vaporized all life on the science station. They even show an altered video of the "event."

Sisko tells Keiko, who bravely insists on seeing this tape. Sisko plans the memorial service while Keiko rushes into his office and declares that the tape is doctored. It shows Miles drinking coffee in the afternoon. She claims he never does so as it keeps him awake.

Sisko dispatches Dax to T'Lani 3 to reclaim the runabout. He decides to join her on this mission.

Significant character development occurs in this episode. Keiko launches the investigation. Julian gives Dax his medical school diaries to read but she's never found the time to read them. She wants to give them back to his parents. Kira suggests she keep and read them.

It seems he has shared more than mere lechery with Dax. She knows what an insecure but ambitious young man he was at Starfleet Medical school. On T'Lani 3, Julian reveals more of his youth to O'Brien. He tells of a woman he once loved but gave up for his career.

Quark shows unexpected sensitivity, toasting the supposedly dead men by saying that they were good customers. This is more than another humorous slant on the Ferengi. It is the highest praise he could give.

The writer of this episode even has Dax and Kira understand this about Quark and accept the toast in the spirit it is intended.

Meanwhile Dax and Sisko arrive at the science station. The two fugitives have opened up to each other. O'Brien's condition is so bad Julian must follow his instructions to get the communication panel working.

At last, they send a signal, only to be greeted by a contingent of soldiers and both ambassadors. Both sides are involved.

A clever plot twist shows that the attack on the science station was not a breach of the treaty. Both sides were so intent on maintaining the peace that they decided to kill everyone who ever had access to the databases on harvester biotechnology, including Bashir and O'Brien. The ambassadors allow O'Brien, already near death, to drag himself to his feet to face their soldiers' guns. This gives them just enough time for Sisko to beam his men up.

The ambassadors beam back to the station to pursue the fleeing Ganges. They jam subspace and sensor signals then order Sisko to surrender his men. Instead he rams a pursuing ship, blowing the Ganges into smithereens.

After the T'Lani and Kelleruns restore sensors, they realize the other runabout is gone. Sisko and his men are on it. They remotely operated the Ganges.

This is a good plot with an unpredictable twist— both sides are behind the attack on the scientists. Sisko uses good tactics. .There's also plenty of effective character development. This includes O'Brien's admission he didn't become a good engineer until the day he had a mere ten minutes to fix a transporter to get himself and other personnel off a base under Cardassian attack. He pulled off the job with seconds to spare.

The dreaded status-quo disease afflicts the end of the episode. While O'Brien recovers in the infirmary, he reverts to his usual gruff self towards Bashir.

The final joke, that he really does drink coffee in the afternoon, falls flat. It doesn't distract from a very good DS9 episode, though.

The viewer is left with a distracting afterthought. The T'Lani and Kelleruns want to destroy all knowledge of the Harvesters. Since it can now be cured, the disease can no longer threaten anyone. The cure renders the weapon useless. A scene should have shown the T'Lani and Kelleruns learning this, whereupon they could have looked at each other in surprise and said, "Never mind. . . ."

WHISPERS

Written by Paul Robert Coyl; Directed by Les Landau

Regular Cast:
Avery Brooks as Commander Benjamin Sisko; Rene Auberjonois as Odo; Siddig El Fadil as Doctor Bashir; Terry Farrell as Lieutenant Dax; Cirroc Lofton as Jake Sisko; Colm Meaney as Chief O'Brien; Armin Shimerman as Quark; Nana Visitor as Major Kira

Guest Stars:
Rosalind Chao as Keiko O'Brien

O'Brien gets the spotlight in "Whispers." The bizarre thriller grips the viewer from the beginning almost to the end. "Whispers" casts the hapless engineer into a world where paranoia is the only possible response.

The story begins as O'Brien returns from the Parada System in the Gamma Quadrant. He had been preparing security arrangements for peace talks between the Parada government and the rebels. The talks will take place on DS9.

Everything appears normal. Everyone is in their proper place, yet something doesn't seem right to Miles. When dinner with his wife and daughter takes a disturbing turn, it's difficult to tell if this is domestic stress or something more sinister.

Tension slowly builds in the early part of this episode. There is question whether O'Brien has gone crazy or if something is very wrong with the DS9 crew justifying his paranoia.

One crew member continues making security arrangements without O'Brien. Commando Sisko assigns him to repair the upper pylons O'Brien overhauled before he left. He soon discovers they have been intentionally disabled.

Sisko and Bashir insist O'Brien take an unscheduled physical. Then he sees his underling entering a secure area he allegedly has no access code to. It begins to appear O'Brien is right to suspect everyone.

O'Brien can no longer access open files of officer's logs for the period after his return, even though his security clearance should allow him access. He breaks through the security lock. Still baffled, he learns there are coded messages from Parada rebels to Sisko.

Finally Sisko and his officers confront O'Brien. They demand he turn himself in. He escapes and steals a runabout.

The station fires on him but the shields hold until he is out of range. He contacts a Starfleet admiral but she tells him to turn himself in.

With no one to turn to, he heads into the wormhole to Gamma Quadrant. He reasons that the answer lies in the Parada System.

It is difficult for an actor to appear on stage alone and maintain a running dialogue for extended periods. Meaney performs very well as he records puzzling events in his personal log. He keeps the story moving and the viewer informed.

He discovers he's followed into the Gamma Quadrant and ditches his pursuer. Hidden from view, he follows them.

Three officers beam down to Parada 2. An armed O'Brien follows, beaming into a cavern and getting the drop on Sisko, Kira and some Paradans. He learns that Sisko and crew have been co-opted by the Paradan rebels.

O'Brien refuses to believe a Paradan who tells him the real answer lies behind a closed door. The news distracts him. He is shot and falls to the ground.

Bashir opens the door and rushes to his aid, followed by another O'Brien. The O'Briens stare at each other. As the wounded "O'Brien" lies dying, the truth is revealed.

The Paradan government wants to sabotage the peace talks and discredit the rebels. They kidnapped O'Brien and replaced him with a replicant programmed as an assassin.

The replicant doesn't know it is a fake. Its dying words reveal its love for "his" wife, Keiko.

Sisko planned to rescue the real O'Brien and prevent the assassination.

This is a fine resolution to this plotline, but painfully derivative. Philip K. Dick wrote this twist years ago. Several of Dick's early stories, including "The Electric Ant," feature androids that believe themselves to be human until the truth is revealed in a final personal apocalypse.

The episode even uses the word "replicant" instead of "android." In print Dick used the word "android," as did many other science fiction writers. The word "replicant" was created to replace "android" in BLADERUNNER, the film based on Dick's novel, DO ANDROIDS DREAM OF ELECTRIC SHEEP?

The conclusion of "Whispers" staggers anyone who has not encountered the idea before. It's a letdown for those who know their science fiction classics.

Replicants, doubles and surgically altered beings are frequently used in science fiction storylines. This is certainly true of STAR TREK.

The original series offered two memorable incidents. Kirk was surgically changed to resemble a Romulan in "The Enterprise Incident." In "Whom Gods Destroy," Garth of Izar, played by Steve Ihnat, has shape-changing powers. He assumes the appearance of a prison director. Later he transforms himself into a double of Kirk.

Doubles also appear in STAR TREK—THE NEXT GENERATION. "Allegiances" features two deceptions. A Picard double assumes his position as captain and an imprisoned Starfleet cadet is unmasked as one of the aliens responsible for his abduction.

Occasionally the double isn't evil. One rare instance occurred in the NEXT GENERATION episode "Second Chances." Riker comes face to face with himself.

Eight years earlier Riker was part of an away team on a planet overwhelmed by a magnetic storm. He was the last to return to the ship. A transporter glitch formed a second Riker who, unknown to anyone, remained on the planet.

The pair of Rikers faced living duplicates with the same feelings, memories and features. Only the eight year gap divided them. In most such situations, the duplicate dies, but not this time.

Lieutenant Thomas Riker found himself eight years behind on his career goals. He dropped his first name, preferring Thomas to William, and accepted a post on another ship. His fate remained undisclosed when the series ended. Perhaps he will show up on DEEP SPACE NINE.

One recent example of a surgically altered duplicate occurred on DEEP SPACE NINE in "Tribunal." A Cardassian spy, played by John Beck, appears human. Considering the extreme differences in the two races, that must have required a very talented team of surgeons.

[Review by Dan Whitworth and Kay Doty]

PARADISE

Written by Jeff King, Richard Manning and Hans Beimler ; Story by Jim Trombette and James Crocker; Directed by Corey Allen

Regular Cast:

Avery Brooks as Commander Benjamin Sisko; Rene Auberjonois as Odo; Siddig El Fadil as Doctor Bashir; Terry Farrell as Lieutenant Dax; Cirroc Lofton as Jake Sisko; Colm Meaney as Chief O'Brien; Armin Shimerman as Quark; Nana Visitor as Major Kira

Guest Stars:

Gail Strickland as Alixus; Steve Vinovich as Joseph

"Paradise" is a pale imitation of Classic STAR TREK. You remember the one with the paradise planet where peace is an undesirable illusion created by a lie.

Sisko and O'Brien discover life on an M-Class planet. They find the crew of a Federation craft that had crashed a decade earlier.

The planet's duonetic field keeps sensors, tricorders and other modern technology from working. Sisko and O'Brien are stranded.

The colony survived under female leadership. They grow crops and defeat disease without 24th Century technology.

The leader views the newcomers as permanent additions to the group. O'Brien suggests that the duonetic field be used as a power source for properly adapted instruments. He is ignored. Soon a struggle of wills begins.

She fails to seduce Sisko when he refuses to remove his uniform. The discovery that the colonists use a sweat box to punish minor transgressions arouses Sisko's disgust.

He is suspicious of the leader. She has written many books. The colony's guiding philosophy follows her social theories.

Sisko can't contact the DS9. Their unmanned runabout is discovered flying through space at low warp speed. Kira and Dax use a "lasso" tractor beam to slow it to impulse speed.

They find the records erased from its computers but trace its trajectory. They learn from radiation traces that someone tried to destroy it by aiming it at a star. They soon head for the proper planet.

Meanwhile O'Brien tries to adapt a communicator to duonetic power. The leader punishes Sisko, his commanding officer, for his actions.

After a session in the sweat box, she offers him water if he will change out of his Starfleet uniform. Sisko refuses. Instead he returns to the sweat box.

Acting on his own and Sisko's suspicions, O'Brien discovers the source of the duonetic field. It is artificial. He disables it in time to reach Dax and Kira.

O'Brien now has an active phaser. He liberates Sisko and returns to the ship with him and the captured leader.

She must face charges for causing the crash. The colonists realize that even if the "accident" was a fake, they have created something worthwhile, and most will stay.

The main conflict in this episode is Sisko's stubborn clash of wills with the leader. The "mystery" of the crash is easy to figure out. O'Brien's discovery of the hidden duonetic field generator is not surprising. Even the decision of the colonists is predictable. Wooden acting makes things worse. This doesn't rate among the best episodes of DEEP SPACE NINE by a long shot.

Sisko appears in an excellent character scene. No one plays stubborn better than Avery Brooks. The contest of wills between Sisko and Alixus is interesting as she realizes she's met her match in this headstrong Starfleet Commander.

Sisko and O'Brien form a less interesting team than O'Brien and Bashir. The location and sound stage scenery provide a welcome break from the dark space station confines.

SHADOWPLAY

Written by Robert Hewitt Wolfe; Directed by Robert Scheerer

Regular Cast:
Avery Brooks as Commander Benjamin Sisko; Rene Auberjonois as Odo; Siddig El Fadil as Doctor Bashir; Terry Farrell as Lieutenant Dax; Cirroc Lofton as Jake Sisko; Colm Meaney as Chief O'Brien; Armin Shimerman as Quark; Nana Visitor as Major Kira

Guest Stars:
Philip Anglim as Vedek Bareil; Kenneth Mars; Kenneth Toby; Noley Thornton

This episode balances two boring on-station subplots with an engaging Gamma Quadrant adventure featuring Odo and Jadzia Dax. The first subplot is minor. It brings simple changes to the Sisko family.

Ben Sisko has always wanted Jake to go to Starfleet Academy. Jake takes a job assisting Miles O'Brien. Jake reveals his doubts to O'Brien while O'Brien reveals a little about his life to Jake. Jake finally tells his father that he doesn't want to go to the Academy. The elder Sisko, as O'Brien predicted, approves.

The second subplot is also weak. Major Kira foils crimes by Quark's cousin Kono, but she can't pin anything on Quark. Bajoran religious leader Vedek Bareil, whom Kira has the hots for, comes to the station to speak at the Bajoran shrine. He and Kira spend time together, slipping towards romance. Then an offhand comment by Bareil, the station's resident cleric, tells Kira that Quark engineered Bareil's visit to distract her.

The cousin is apprehended, but, as usual, Quark looks clean. This slow plotline pads the main story.

The main plot focuses on Odo and Dax. It is not enough to fill an entire episode.

Odo and Dax trace an odd particle field in the Gamma Quadrant to a seemingly uninhabited planet. Scans reveal no life until they beam down to an inhabited village. A reactor is the source of the field.

The village Protector, Kolius, acts friendly but suspicious. Villagers have been vanishing. Odo and Dax win Kolius' trust and promise to help.

The daughter of the oldest man in the village is the latest disappearance. Her father seems oddly uncaring. He's the last of the village's founders.

Thea leads Odo and Dax to the edge of the village. The sensor device borrowed from Kolius disappears once they pass a certain point. They are unaffected but Thea's arm vanishes, then reappears when she pulls it back.

Dax learns the reactor is a holographic projector. The village and its inhabitants are holograms. One of the reactor's components is breaking down, causing the disappearances.

When the reactor is shut down, everything disappears. Only the old man remains. He tells Dax and Odo that he fled his home world when a repressive government took over and then created his holographic home.

The village is restored. The Deep Space Nine crew keep the old man's secret.

This main story works well, but the patched-together subplots make "Shadowplay" a mixed bag. The episode raises issues originally brought up in NEXT GENERATION storylines.

Computer generated, 24th Century holograms appear to have personalities and a sense of self. Holograms may be a form of life. It has been seven years since "The Big Goodbye" first introduced living holograms. They've danced around the concept ever since without a definitive statement.

Odo and Dax relate better to people on the world than they do to each other. There is little character play between them.

They are the two most unusual regulars on DEEP SPACE NINE. Odo is a shape-shifter from the Gamma Quadrant and Dax is a Trill, a joining of two different beings. Neither has much in common with their associates, although Dax tries to be sociable.

In the episode "Profit And Loss" Quark questions whether Odo understands love. In "Shadowplay" he Odo seems taken with the little girl, revealing a gentle emotional side.

The viewer wonders about the fate of this village after the Dominion closed the wormhole in "The Jem 'Hedar." The colony of New Bajor was wiped out, but how did other worlds fare? And what is the fate of the old man who had already fled from oppressors who had destroyed his society?

PLAYING GOD

Written by Jim Trombetta and Michael Piller; Story by Jim Trombetta; Directed by David Livingston

Regular Cast:
Avery Brooks as Commander Benjamin Sisko; Rene Auberjonois as Odo; Siddig El Fadil as Doctor Bashir; Terry Farrell as Lieutenant Dax; Cirroc Lofton as Jake Sisko; Colm Meaney as Chief O'Brien; Armin Shimerman as Quark; Nana Visitor as Major Kira

Guest Stars:
Geoffrey Blake; Ron Taylor; Richard Poe; Chris Nelson Norris

Dax gets the least attention of any DS9 regular. This episode focuses on her. This time we learn what it means to be a Trill.

A shuttle docks at space station Deep Space Nine. Argen disembarks.

He's been training to become a Trill. Five thousand candidates qualify each year. There are only 300 available symbionts.

This adds new information about the Trills. It still doesn't reveal where the symbionts come from, what their culture is like or even how the Trill program began.

Argen meets Dax. She leaves a Tongo game she is playing with Ferengi.

Argen is surprised at Dax's quarters when an alien tells him she is in the shower. Dax walks out wearing a towel and remarks, "It was fun; brutal but fun." This is the first time the series has shown a personal life is shown for Dax.

Another first is the revelation that the space station is infested with Cardassian voles. They are small creatures attracted by electromagnetic fields. When the Cardassians left the station they didn't exterminate them. Perhaps it was a parting gift to the Federation.

A subplot is introduced when the runabout runs into trouble. It is meant to prop up the storyline. The characterization of Dax and Argen isn't interesting enough to sustain the hour. The damaged nacelle on the runabout snags a miniature universe in a subspace pocket.

Meanwhile O'Brien and Kira discuss a way to get rid of the voles. O'Brien shows Quark a sonic device to use against the voles. When he turns it on, Quark screams and collapses. When the device is turned off, he has no memory of what happened. O'Brien has found a way to get rid of Ferengi as well as voles. This could prove significant in future stories.

Background on Argen finally emerges. He admits he joined the program because it was his father's dying wish. He says he expects the Symbiont to guide him.

Dax warns that if the host personality is too weak, they won't merge. The symbiont will dominate and the host personality will be completely submerged.

Dax tells Sisko the proto-universe will grow and displace our universe. She doesn't know if they can safely take it back through the wormhole. Sisko suggests a containment field to force the mass to collapse upon itself.

A probe in the science lab reveals life in the proto-universe. The universe expands and breeches the station hull. Kira wants to destroy it but Odo doesn't. Sisko must decide.

Ben learns that Jake has a girlfriend, the Dabo girl he has been tutoring. Ben first objects and then accepts this. His emotions run hot and cold fast. The nature of a Dabo girl has never been revealed. The viewer is left to make up their own mind whether she's a waitress or something more.

Dax talks to Argen about Jadzia. She was brilliant but shy. When Curzon tried to have her dismissed from the program she fought hard to improve herself, and even applied for Dax when Curzon was dying. He accepted her.

Oddly Dax says she doesn't know why. If Jadzia and Dax now share memories she should know exactly why. This is a strange inconsistency in the story.

Dax and Argen take the proto-universe through the wormhole. The containment field erodes inside the wormhole. They halt the shuttle to avoid vitrion nodes but finally return the mass to the subspace pocket.

After returning to the station, Argen and Dax discuss joining. She decides to recommend Argen and when he leaves she says, "I'm not Curzon," meaning that Jadzia's personality is very different from what Curzon had brought to the joining.

This rare Dax episode offers only brief personality scenes. It would have been more interesting if she walked Argen through her life or had him sit in with the Ferengi when she played Tongo so he could interact with an alien culture.

Argen appears devoid of significant life experiences. Dax questions what he would bring to a joining.

When Jadzia gave Julian Bashir the brush-off, this made her appear sexless. That's clearly not the case. In "The Maquis," one of Sisko's friends inquires whether he's involved with Jadzia since she's beautiful and Sisko and Curzon Dax had been close friends.

This episode only hints at the possibilities for character development with Dax.

PROFIT AND LOSS

Written by Flip Kobler and Cindy Marcus; Directed by Robert Wiemer

Regular Cast:
Avery Brooks as Commander Benjamin Sisko; Rene Auberjonois as Odo; Siddig El Fadil as Doctor Bashir; Terry Farrell as Lieutenant Dax; Cirroc Lofton as Jake Sisko; Colm Meaney as Chief O'Brien; Armin Shimerman as Quark; Nana Visitor as Major Kira

Guest Stars:
Mary Crosby as Prof. Natima Lang; Andrew Robinson as Garak; Michael Reilly Burke; Heidi Swedberg; Edward Wiley

Mary Crosby appears in this episode as Prof. Natima Lang. She is the sister of Denise Crosby, who played Tasha Yar on STAR TREK—THE NEXT GENERATION. In this episode she plays the object of Quark's affections. She was once Quark's lover!

A Cardassian shuttle is detected approaching Deep Space Nine. The shuttle is damaged so a tractor beam pulls it into cargo bay 7. The passengers, three Cardassians, disembark.

They are Prof. Natima Lang and two of her students. She wants to repair her ship and then be on her way.

Odo and Quark discuss a small cloaking device he's heard Quark acquired. He says it is illegal under Bajoran law and vows to arrest Quark if he tries to sell it.

According to THE NEXT GENERATION episode "Pegasus," the Federation prohibits experimenting with cloaking technology because of the Romulan treaty. Only Klingon ships may be so equipped in the Federation. The technology must be popular on the black market.

Suddenly Quark sees Natima. He runs to her, but she slaps his face and tells him she doesn't want him near her.

Quark offers her a drink, a Sumerian Sunset that she used to love. She doesn't want to drink them because they remind her of him.

Quark tells Odo that seven years before Natima had worked on the station as a correspondent for the Cardassian Information Service. Quark claims he was the love of her life. Odo finds it hard to believe.

Natima has a Sumerian Sunset. When she sees Garak enter the bar, she abruptly leaves with her two students. She didn't know other Cardassians were on the station.

O'Brien works on Natima's ship. He discovers that the damage is from disrupter fire. Natima says that unless she and her students leave soon, the Cardassians will kill them. They are in the anti-military underground.

This is the first mention of political factions on Cardassia Prime in the series. In the first season episode "Duet," the late Aamin Marritza seemed to be a very singular Cardassian in that

166 ■ **DEEP SPACE**

166 ■ **DEEP SPACE**

he felt anguish and guilt over what his people had perpetrated on the Bajorans. Now it is revealed that the Cardassian military doesn't command the complete popular support of the people.

Quark wants to help Natima. Natima and Quark had a falling out seven years before. They met when Quark sold food to the Bajorans. He went too far, using her personal access code to bill the Cardassians for goods he never delivered. They had been lovers for a month when Quark's greed got the best of him. Natima finds it difficult to trust Quark.

She tells Quark that she has to stay with her students. He says he'll go with them. She doesn't believe that this would work because Quark is too selfish. They mouth clichés in this love scene, including Quark saying, "Now which one of us is lying?" If the participants weren't aliens, the silliness of the dialogue would be apparent.

A Cardassian warship approaches.

Garak tells Sisko that Natima's students are terrorists. Sisko won't turn them over to Cardassian Central Command. He promises that if the Cardassians use force then so will the space station and puts the station on full alert.

Quark tells the students he can help them get away. He will give them a cloaking device as a gift if they persuade Natima to stay with him. Quark is uncharacteristically honest and admits that the device isn't in good shape and will only function for 15 minutes. This honesty doesn't fit Quark as he's usually portrayed.

Natima insists she won't stay behind. This is a silly, cliché good-bye scene different only because it's between two aliens. She pulls a gun on Quark and demands the cloaking device.

She shoots him by accident, but is not seriously hurt. Natima says, "I love you. I always loved you," and kisses him. Perhaps Armin Shimmerman paid them to write this scrip. If it was meant as parody, that would be one thing. It doesn't come across as a parody, though.

Quark makes love with Natima. She says she has "responsibilities," and even says, "we did have fun together, didn't we?" recalling old times on the holodeck. "You painted my face with honey." And a butterfly got stuck on her nose. Says Quark, "His wings were beating almost as fast as my heart." But Natima doesn't want to abandon the anti-military movement.

Odo arrests Prof. Lang because the Bajoran Provisional Government has made a deal with the Cardassians. Sisko opposes to it but Deep Space Nine is a Bajoran station. There's nothing he can do.

Another Cardassian, Gul Turan, arrives to see Garak. They are old adversaries. This scene shows that Garak is in exile from Cardassia.

Gul Turan tells Garak to make sure the prisoners die before leaving the station. Turan has persuaded the Cardassians not to go ahead with the prisoner exchange. Garak agrees as this will get him back into the good graces of the Cardassian Central Command.

Quark pleads with Odo for the prisoners. They could help open Cardassian society.

Odo knows the real reason behind Quark's request. He is perplexed by the whole business and Quark accuses Odo of being incapable of feelings. Odo doesn't dispute him.

Is Odo emotionless? This hasn't been established previously. Odo expresses anger and annoyance, but what about love? This has yet to be explored. So far we've seen Bashir, Sisko, Kira, O'Brien and Quark in love, but not Odo.

Odo finally releases the prisoners. His investigations reveal they've not committed a crime.

The prisoners are about to leave when an armed Garak confronts them. He reveals his plans to kill them so he can return to Cardassia. Natima tells him this won't matter as Cardassia is already slipping away from the military.

Garak admits this may be true. This is a new revelation in the series. Not only is there a Cardassian anti-military underground on the home world but it is succeeding in destabilizing the regime.

Gul Turan arrives brandishing a gun. He doesn't trust Garak. Turan disarms Garak, but he has another hidden gun that he uses to disintegrate Turan.

This is the first time someone is disintegrated on DEEP SPACE NINE. Previously phasers were only used to stun.

What other settings are available on phasers can only be guessed. The NEXT GENERATION episode "Preemptive Strike" showed a man shot by a Cardassian. The setting doesn't disintegrate but it does kill.

Garak allows the prisoners to leave. Natima tells Quark she has to go, but she'll be back when Cardassia is free. She says she'll make it worth the wait to Quark.

She won't let Quark come because she'd never forgive herself if anything happened to him. This is a very cliched good-bye scene.

Several new items are added in this episode. The most significant new aspect is the introduction of the Cardassian anti-military underground.

BLOOD OATH

Written by Peter Allan Fields; Directed by Winrich Kolbe

Regular Cast:

Avery Brooks as Commander Benjamin Sisko; Rene Auberjonois as Odo; Siddig El Fadil as Doctor Bashir; Terry Farrell as Lieutenant Dax; Cirroc Lofton as Jake Sisko; Colm Meaney as Chief O'Brien; Armin Shimerman as Quark; Nana Visitor as Major Kira

Guest Stars:

John Colicos as Kor; Michael Ansara as Kang; William Campbell as Koloth; Bill Bolender; Christopher Collins

Klingons occassionally appear on DEEP SPACE NINE. They never feature as major characters. A Klingon chef runs a restaurant in "Melora," something Kang refers to with derision in "Blood Oath." The first season episode, "Dramatis Personae," shows a Klingon briefly in the episode teaser.

Neither episode reveals anything about the character. They each only appear in one scene. It seemed Klingons were exclusive to STAR TREK—THE NEXT GENERATION. All that changed in this episode. It equals the best Klingon episodes of THE NEXT GENERATION.

A drunk, screaming Klingon named Kor pulls open the doors of the holosuite. He then passes out in a holding cell.

John Colicos delivers a marvelous performance, playing Kor as a Falstaffian character. Kor is loud, boisterous and good-natured. Unlike Falstaff, the Klingon is a proud and fearless warrior. Colicos first played Kor in the original STAR TREK episode "Errand of Mercy." That story introduced the Klingons to the STAR TREK mythos.

Odo is surprised by another Klingon. He demands to know how he got in. The Klingon only replies, "I am Koloth."

Koloth is taken to Kor. He expresses anger at finding the man drunk in a holding cell.

William Campbell played Koloth in the original STAR TREK episode "The Trouble With Tribbles," in the second season. There were discussions about bringing Koloth back in episodes for the third season. When Gene Roddenberry stepped down as producer, plans to further use Koloth were dropped. Campbell played a completely different character, Trelane, in the first season of the original STAR TREK in the episode "Squire of Gothos."

Odo tells Major Kira about his Klingon afternoon. When he mentions Kor, Dax knows of him. She accompanies Odo to the holding cell and takes charge of Kor.

Dax asks Kor if he remembers Curzon Dax. She convinces him that is who she once was. Kor is surprised and amused.

It is easy to see why John Colicos got top billing of the three guest stars. Kor has all the best scenes and the actor delivers an excellent character performance.

They meet Koloth and Dax introduces herself. An angry Koloth insists this is a mistake. Kang arrives and announces he has found the Albino.

Michael Ansara first played Kang in the original STAR TREK episode "Day Of The Dove." Ansara is known for appearances in other science fiction stories including as Quarlo in THE OUTER LIMITS episode "Soldier," written by Harlan Ellison, as well as in the 1960 motion picture VOYAGE TO THE BOTTOM OF THE SEA.

Kang resists the idea that Jadzia is Dax. She insists she is still the godfather of his son, the same Dax who took a blood oath with them 81 years before. She warns, "Don't mistake a new face for a new soul." This reminds the viewer that Dax has a long history, passing through many lives.

Kang vows to find and kill the Albino. Dax appears troubled.

Kang is disappointed to learn Curzon died in a hospital. He feels Curzon deserved a warrior's death. The story thus illustrates the Klingon philosophy. It looks down on doctors and hospitals. Klingons prefer to die in battle rather then live as a cripple. This is also shown in the NEXT GENERATION episode "Ethics."

Kang bemoans the passing of the old Klingon ways. He observes that Klingons are opening restaurants to serve the grandchildren of men he slaughtered in battle. This reflects the significant difference in the role of Klingons in classic STAR TREK and 24th Century STAR TREK. The Federation's implacable enemies have now become allies.

Dax asks Kira what it is like to kill, then explains the reason for her question. This scene allows the character internal development by bringing her basic values into conflict. Dax intends to kill someone responsible for the deaths of three children but questions whether even such a person's life is worthy of respect.

Klingons may be casual about taking life, but Dax weighs the opposite extreme and wonders if she can take a life. She also questions whether she has the right to take the law into her own hands.

Kor supports Dax's willingness to come with them. He says Koloth and Kang oppose her involvement.

The viewer wonders who will survive this escapade. The series regular Dax clearly won't die, but the three Klingons might.

Koloth practices with the Klingon Bat'Leth sword. He insists Dax's presence will jeopardize the mission. She duels him to prove her worth. Koloth wins but admits her mettle as a warrior.

A stunt man is used for much of this sequence. Koloth is shown doing swift movements only from the rear. During the fight his face is often obscured. Under the Klingon make-up you need a medium shot to recognize him and the fight is mostly in long shots.

Dax baits Kang into anger. Finally he shouts, "Come and fight with us. Come and be damned!" This scene is intended to show that Klingons often make decisions from hot emotion rather than logic.

Dax is preparing to leave when Sisko abruptly enters. Major Kira has informed him of Dax's plans. He forbids Dax to take a leave of absence pointing out Federation laws against killing and that she is a Federation officer.

Dax explains that to Klingons this is justice. Sisko responds both out of duty as commanding officer and friendship for Dax. Jadzia remains unmoved. She tells Ben he can decide whether she can return to duty after this is over.

This scene both illustrates the bond between Dax and Sisko and the differences between Klingons and the Federation. Legal procedure may be important to the starship captain, but honor is primary to a Klingon.

The comrades embark on a Klingon bird of prey. Kang wants a direct attack. Dax points out it would be a suicide mission. Kang admits that the Albino contacted him and offered the chance for final battle against 40 of his guards.

Kang believes this is their last chance. Dax says an honorable victory is better than an honorable defeat, but Kang doesn't believe there's any chance for victory.

This story gives Dax important scenes. She now creates a plan to neutralize the Albino's weapons. It will give them a chance to penetrate the walls of his sanctuary.

The science officer knows their vessel can neutralize all the Albino's energy weapons. Curzon the diplomat wouldn't have had this knowledge. Thus the story reveals something Jadzia brought to the joining with Dax.

They arrive at the planet and discover that the Albino had planted a bomb at the place he agreed to fight the Klingons. There never was to be a true battle. They hatch an alternate plan.

Dax blows up the armory, creating a diversion while the Klingons attack elsewhere. Kor, Koloth, Kang and Dax fight their way into the stronghold, cutting down guards unaccustomed to facing a Bat'Leth-wielding Klingon.

Koloth is struck down. Kor goes to his friend and, as Koloth dies, tells him he'll sing the story of Koloth's courage to Klingon children.

Kang fights his way to the Albino. They duel. The Albino mortally wounds Kang. Before the Albino can finish the job, Dax disarms him. The Albino challenges her to kill him.

Dax hesitates, giving Kang the chance to stab the Albino in the back with his dying strength. Kang thanks Dax, believing she hesitated to allow him to deliver the death blow to his mortal enemy.

"I was right," Kang gasps, "It is a good day to die."

As Kang dies, Dax says, "It's never a good day to lose a friend." Kor utters the Klingon death chant.

Dax returns to the space station and resumes her duties. Kira and Sisko silently wonder if Dax ate the heart of the dead Albino as her oath commanded. Certainly Kor would have completed the oath.

Upon first viewing this episode the final scene seems strangely detached and remote. Watching it again you see there's a drawn and tight expression on Dax's face. She's clearly upset by everything she went through and so the others back off.

Some viewers believe Dax failed to learn anything from the experience because it isn't spelled out in the last scene. No one says anything to Dax and she says nothing when she returns to duty.

This is the whole point. She's overwhelmed by her experience. Two old friends died in front of her. She was faced with having to kill in cold blood and learned she couldn't do it.

She fought well but it isn't clear how badly she wounded the guards. When she faced the Albino, he was unarmed. Her blood oath still demanded he be slain.

Klingons previously seen on STAR TREK were younger with the exception of Kahless in "Rightful Heir." Kor, Koloth and Kang are all supposed to be more than a hundred years old. This is an interesting departure.

This fine episode is easily one of the five best in the first two seasons of DEEP SPACE NINE.

THE MAQUIS, PART I

Written by James Crocker; Story by Rick Berman & Michael Piller & Jeri Taylor and James Crocker; Directed by David Livingston

Regular Cast:
Avery Brooks as Commander Benjamin Sisko; Rene Auberjonois as Odo; Siddig El Fadil as Doctor Bashir; Terry Farrell as Lieutenant Dax; Cirroc Lofton as Jake Sisko; Colm Meaney as Chief O'Brien; Armin Shimerman as Quark; Nana Visitor as Major Kira

Guest Stars:
Marc Alaimo as Gul Dukat; Bernie Casey as Calvin Hudson; Michael Rose as Niles; Steven John Evans as Guard; Tony Plana; Bertila Damas; Richard Poe; Michael A. Krawic; Amanda Carlin

This key episode of DEEP SPACE NINE appeared late in the second season. It changed both DEEP SPACE NINE and STAR TREK—THE NEXT GENERATION.

The last few episodes of the second season set up the fireworks for the third season of DEEP SPACE NINE. The creators obviously want to keep attention focused on this series now that the more dynamic STAR TREK—THE NEXT GENERATION has ended its original TV run. Without TNG to ride along on, DEEP SPACE NINE has to stand on its own. It must now explore new territory rather than covering the same ground as before.

Someone quietly slips aboard a Cardassian vessel docked at Deep Space Nine. They tamper with a wall panel.

Meanwhile Dax tells Kira she is having dinner with a Galamite. Kira is surprised because Galamites have transparent skulls.

This is an example of the vast experience gained in Dax's previous lives and how they have an impact on her present one. She is untroubled dealing with such a being, seeing their brain while eating dinner with them.

The Cardassian ship barely leaves the docking bay before exploding. The explosion destroys the ship and kills more than 70 crewmen as O'Brien and Kira watch.

They try to pinpoint the cause. Commander Sisko is under pressure to learn if it is sabotage. The Cardassians plan reprisals.

Dax discovers evidence of sabotage.

Commander Calvin Hudson, the Federation attaché to the colonies in the Demilitarized Zone, arrives on Deep Space Nine. He's an old friend of Sisko and knows Dax from the old days.

Hudson believes the Federation abandoned their colonies with the Cardassian treaty. He believes the Cardassians work behind the scenes to undermine the colony. He assures Sisko that the Cardassians won't send forces into the Demilitarized Zone as they're less overt than that.

Sisko doesn't agree.

Meanwhile a Vulcan woman arrives on the station. She contacts a man without drawing attention to herself. This is a rare appearance of a Vulcan on DEEP SPACE NINE. Despite the number of Vulcans in the original STAR TREK, they have only rarely been seen in 24th Century STAR TREK. They became more frequent guests in the later seasons of NEXT GENERATION due to the appearances of Sarek and Spock.

The Vulcan wants to do business with Quark. He acts defensive because he's had poor dealings with Vulcans in the past, but hastens to add that he's willing to wipe the slate clean. This would be to Quark's advantage. He was most likely responsible for past bad dealings, not the Vulcans.

The Vulcan woman's name is Secona. They agree to meet for dinner. Quark hopes to get the Vulcan woman interested in him, something even more unlikely than getting a non-Vulcan woman interested in him. The latter proved successful in the episode "Profit And Loss."

A man is overpowered and dragged off but later turns up in the hands of the Cardassians. Humans must have turned the man over to the Cardassians.

Commander Sisko finds Gul Dukat in his quarters and demands to know how he got in. He didn't even know that the Cardassian was aboard the station.

Dukat admits he arrived as an unregistered passenger on a cargo ship. He's there in secret to discuss the problems in the Demilitarized Zone.

Marc Alaimo again plays Gul Dukat. He has played this recurring role since the first DEEP SPACE NINE episode, "Emissary."

Dukat says the Cardassians believe the Maquis, a group of renegade Federation colonists, attacked the freighter. Dukat wants Sisko to deal with events in the colonies so the Cardassians don't have to get involved.

Sisko agrees to go to the colonies. He and Dukat leave the space station. En route they discuss the Cardassian education system, which begins mind-training a child at age 4. This adds background on the Cardassians. It will also play a role in the story in part two of "The Maquis."

Sisko remarks that they take all the fun out of childhood. Dukat quickly replies, "Education is power, joy is vulnerability."

Despite such lines, Gul Dukat seems more trustworthy than the Maquis in this episode. Dukat never seemed trustworthy before. Amusingly he follows the line about joy being vulnerability with the observation that Sisko is the most joyless and least vulnerable human he's ever met. That's an apt observation of the stony-faced Sisko.

Their long-range scanners pick up a distress signal from a Federation vessel under attack from two small Cardassian ships. Dukat orders the ships to break off their attack but they ignore him. Before the runabout can reach the scene, another Federation ship destroys the two Cardassian ships. Dukat points out that the Cardassian and Federation colonists have begun fighting a private war.

On the space station Quark meets the Vulcan for dinner. They discuss business and Quark explains that Ferengi have 285 Rules of Acquisition. The Vulcan finds this logical, comparing it to the Vulcan bill of rights. This story bit doesn't illuminate very much and is rather boring.

Quark wants to impress this Vulcan woman with more than business. He is taken aback when she wants to buy phaser banks, photon torpedoes and cobalt thorium. This closely follows Sisko and Dukat noticing that the ships engaged in the dogfight in the Demilitarized Zone were unusually well armed for such small vessels.

The surprised Quark doesn't refuse. He lamely remarks, "You're not like other Vulcans, are you?"

In a Federation colony people argue about the attack on the Federation merchant ship. Two Cardassians claim the vessel was attacked when it refused to be boarded for inspection. They insist it was transporting unauthorized armaments.

It is impossible to decide who the instigators are and who the victims. Perhaps both sides are to blame?

Hudson argues with Gul Evek. Gul Evek was also seen in "Preemptive Strike" when Picard saved his life from the Maquis.

Gul Dukat and Ben Sisko visit the colony then return to Deep Space Nine. Along the way they argue about whether the Cardassians are arming the colonists.

During the argument, Gul Dukat says he has seven children. It is odd to see this Cardassian, portrayed as an unrepentant villain for almost forty episodes, suddenly shown to have a compassionate side.

The Vulcan wants weapons from Quark. The Ferengi agrees to move up the time table. She says she finds Quark intriguing, making the Ferengi happy. He thinks he has a chance with the Vulcan.

In Ops Sisko is told that a Federation implosive device blew up the Cardassian ship. Federation colonists are to blame. Kira defends the colonists. She recalls living under Cardassians for 26 years and doesn't trust them. This story point underlines the history of this character as a member of the undergound which finally forced the Cardassians off their planet.

Elsewhere on the station, the Vulcan woman and a human lure Gul Dukat from his quarters. He is kidnapped.

Odo is furious, claiming his hands are tied with Federation rules and regulations. Kira complains that Odo would run the station just as the Cardassians did. Odo points out that the station was safer then. "Untie my hands!" Odo pleads angrily.

Odo was originally appointed head of security on the space station by Gul Dukat, as shown in "Necessary Evil." He is well aware of life on Deep Space Nine then and now. Although retained by the Federation when they took over the station, Odo always seems as much at arm's length from the Federation as he was from the Cardassians.

Odo has no friends. His relationship with Kira was strained when he discovered she'd been keeping a secret from him for five years, even after he'd saved her life by never revealing to Gul Dukat that she was a Bajoran terrorist.

The Maquis take credit for kidnapping Gul Dukat. Sisko tracks the ship to an area of the Demilitarized Zone called "The Badlands." Sisko, Bashir and Kira go to a class M asteroid and are almost immediately taken prisoner by the Maquis led by Calvin Hudson, Ben Sisko's old friend.

That Hudson is a Maquis is no real surprise. He was the only guest star given dimension. The show carefully showed his friendship with Ben Sisko and painted a mutual background going back years. It was clear writers were setting him up to look like a straightforward guy who played by the rules.

The Maquis are introduced in this episode. They become an important supporting element, particularly in the NEXT GENERATION episode "Preemptive Strike." The Maquis will also play a role in STAR TREK: VOYAGER, the new series set to premiere in 1995.

END OF PART ONE

THE MAQUIS, PART II

Written by Ira Steven Behr; Story by Rick Berman & Michael Piller & Jeri Taylor and Ira Steven Behr; Directed by Corey Allen;

Regular Cast:
Avery Brooks as Commander Benjamin Sisko; Rene Auberjonois as Odo; Siddig El Fadil as Doctor Bashir; Terry Farrell as Lieutenant Dax; Cirroc Lofton as Jake Sisko; Colm Meaney as Chief O'Brien; Armin Shimerman as Quark; Nana Visitor as Major Kira

Guest Stars:
Marc Alaimo as Gul Dukat; Bernie Casey as Calvin Hudson; Michael Rose as Niles; John Schuck; Tony Plana; Bertila Damas; Michael Bell; Amanda Carlin

The second part of the story reveals more about the Maquis and their grievances against the Cardassians. Key events uncover facts and blur the lines. It's not clear which group reacted and which provoked. The Federation colonists seem bigoted against Cardassians. THE NEXT GENERATION episode "Preemptive Strike" reveals more about the Maquis on a personal level.

Ben Sisko and the others are surrounded by the Maquis when they beam down. Sisko is surprised to see his friend, Calvin Hudson, with the Maquis.

Hudson says he can accomplish more fighting alongside the settlers than as a Federation attaché. The Federation thinks they can solve every problem with a treaty, but on the frontier a treaty is just paper.

Sisko opposes the violent tactics of the Maquis. He says, "You don't want peace, Cal, you want revenge." Sisko and Hudson no longer see eye to eye. When the Maquis prepare to leave, they stun Sisko, Kira and Bashir.

Aboard Deep Space Nine a Federation admiral presses Sisko for results. When she leaves and Kira enters, Sisko explodes, complaining that the Federation doesn't understand what he contends with.

This is the scene in which Sisko states, "On Earth there is no poverty, no crime, no war." This continues Gene Roddenberry's optimistic view of the future. Sisko concludes, "It's easy to be a saint in paradise, but the Maquis don't live in paradise."

Ben Sisko and Calvin Hudson are not that far apart; only their methods differ. Sisko knows the Federation high command doesn't understand the problems of the settlers. This illustrates a previously ignored division between those who settle the frontiers of space and those who stay closer to home in the universe of STAR TREK.

Odo arrests Quark for helping supply weapons to the Maquis. Quark explains that Vulcans appreciate good ears. Sisko demands to know what Quark sold Secona. He admits selling her 200 photon torpedoes and he offers to supply a list. He insists he knew nothing of the Maquis until Gul Dukat was kidnapped.

The writers add an amusing touch when Odo asks Sisko how long to lock Quark up. Ben replies, "Forever." Quark isn't sure if Sisko is joking.

It's no wonder Sisko isn't happy to find himself in the forced company of Quark in the season finale, "The Jem 'Hedar."

A member of the Cardassian Central Command, played by John Schuck, arrives at the space station. He informs Commander Sisko that Gul Dukat was supplying arms to the settlers. The Central Command doesn't want him retrieved.

Previously in STAR TREK Cardassia always tried criminals in showcase trials after first convicting them ahead of time. One such trial occurred in "Tribunal." The Cardassian promptly leaves the station. Sisko just as promptly decides not to trust him. He believes the Cardassian settlers were supplied weapons by Central Command just as the Maquis claimed.

Odo, Bashir and Sisko figure out how to find Dukat. Kira wants to leave Gul Dukat to the not-so-tender mercies of the Maquis. Sisko decides that if Central Command wants Dukat dead, then that's a perfect reason to bring him back alive.

The Maquis have Dukat and the Vulcan, Secona. She tries to mind-meld with the Cardassian. The Vulcan fails because Cardassians undergo strict mind control training from the age of four. This is a very different experience than Vulcans usually encounter.

Odo, Bashir and Sisko arrive in time to prevent sterner measures from being employed on Dukat. Sisko doesn't want a fight but Dukat forces the issue by attacking his captors. The Maquis lose. The last one is captured when Odo turns his arm into a tentacle. Everyone returns to the space station.

Gul Dukat enjoys his first meal since capture as Commander Sisko visits. Dukat tries to be friendly but Ben won't join in. Dukat wonders why Cardassian ships didn't surround the space station after his kidnapping. Sisko reveals that the Cardassian Central Command think Dukat is involved in arms smuggling. Dukat is disturbed that he has fallen into disfavor with Central Command.

He admits Central Command must be behind the weapons smuggling. Dukat offers to help stop the smuggling if Sisko will stop the Maquis. He believes Zeppelites act as middlemen so they track down a Zeppelite ship.

Dukat, Kira and Sisko approach the ship. It won't allow them to board. Dukat steps in, insisting they be allowed on board and that the captain sign a confession implicating Central Command.

The Zeppelite is confused because a Cardassian is giving the orders. He complies. This puts Dukat back into a position of strength with Central Command. He now has the confession to hang over their heads.

Quark and Secona share a cell on the space station. Quark convinces the Vulcan that peace can be bought at a bargain price. She reveals the Maquis plan to attack a weapons depot in a civilian center in the Cardassian colonies. Sisko knows this will bring war.

Sisko goes to the Federation colonies to confront the Maquis revealing to Hudson that he knows of the impending attack. He insists Cardassian arms smuggling has been halted.

Hudson and the Maquis are no longer interested in merely halting the arms shipments. They want to force the Cardassians out of the frontier. These raids lead to the actions of the Cardassians in "Tribunal."

Aboard the space station, Sisko and Dukat argue whether the Maquis can be stopped non-violently. Dukat accompanies Sisko in one runabout while Kira and Bashir ride in another. Three runabouts lie in wait for the two Maquis ships. The Maquis are poorly supplied and can use only two ships for a major raid.

A dogfight follows in which all the vessels try only to disable each other. Sisko and Hudson are fight. The Maquis must get past these ships to make their raid, but neither side wants to kill the other.

Dukat wants to crush the Maquis but Sisko refuses to kill a good man for defending his home. Sisko lets them escape.

The Maquis will strike again unless Dukat removes the weapons from the colonies. This story thread is left dangling. Sisko admits he didn't prevent a war so much as delay it.

Future stories will make this evident, including the NEXT GENERATION episode, "Preemptive Strike." It aired a month after the Maquis were introduced on DEEP SPACE NINE.

THE WIRE

Written by Robert Hewitt Wolfe; Directed by Kim Friedman

Regular Cast:
Avery Brooks as Commander Benjamin Sisko; Rene Auberjonois as Odo; Siddig El Fadil as Doctor Bashir; Terry Farrell as Lieutenant Dax; Cirroc Lofton as Jake Sisko; Colm Meaney as Chief O'Brien; Armin Shimerman as Quark; Nana Visitor as Major Kira

Guest Stars:
Andrew Robinson as Garak; Paul Dooley as Enabran Tain; Jimmie F. Skaggs; Ann Gillespie

Garak poses a conundrum since he was introduced in the first season of DEEP SPACE NINE. The last remaining Cardassian in residence on the space station runs a clothing shop and claims to be nothing more than a simple tailor. This episode shows that he is more than that.

"Profit And Loss" previously showed that Garak is an exile from Cardassia. No more was revealed. This episode finally uncovers more.

Dr. Bashir and Garak have been friends for a year and a half. Whether they trust each other is not clear.

In "Cardassians" Garak helped Dr. Bashir uncover information implicating Gul Dukat in a crime. This demonstrated that Garak did not hold the former military regent of Bajor in high esteem. This time Garak doesn't control the situation.

Garak and Dr. Bashir talk as they wait in line at a restaurant. They eat lunch together once a week.

Garak recently gave Dr. Bashir a Cardassian novel called THE NEVER-ENDING SACRI-FICE. Julian describes it as a story of several generations in a Cardassian family leading selfless lives devoted to the state. It is the same story over and over again. Garak explains that the repetitive epic is common in Cardassian literature. One wonders if this was true before the military took over the government. The military promotes the concept that the state is more important than the individual.

"There's more to life than duty to the state," Dr. Bashir observes. Garak finds this typical of Federation thinking. He believes Bashir has been brainwashed into this.

Garak likes the Cardassian status quo and is clearly unhappy to be excluded from it. This is explored in detail, but more in general than specifics.

When Garak suffers from a headache he rushes off rather than allow Julian to examine him. This strikes the doctor as strange.

Dr. Bashir's skills are revealed in other areas when he determines what's wrong with a strange plant. She called in Julian for help because Keiko O'Brien, the botanist, is off-station. Keiko seems to be off-station a lot in this series.

Later Julian observes Garak meeting with Quark and overhears some of their conversation. Garak has never dealt with Quark. Now he wants the Ferengi to obtain a certain piece of "merchandise" for him. Garak worries Quark will fail.

Julian is suspicious and talks to O'Brien about accessing the old Cardassian medical files. This would take weeks with no guarantee of success.

Dr. Bashir is summoned to Quark's place because Garak is acting drunk and disorderly. The Ferengi knows that Julian is Garak's friend. Garak complains about a headache and then collapses. The episode shows how emergency transfers to the infirmary work when Bashir has himself and Garak beamed there.

A scan of Garak reveals that the Cardassian has an implant in his brain. When Julian asks Odo if he knows about this, the security chief says he does not. Garak is still unconscious.

Bashir thinks Quark might know something. He tells Odo about the clandestine meeting he witnessed between Garak and the Ferengi.

Odo and Julian listen when Quark puts through a call to his contact on Cardassia. The communication is friendly. Quark requests Cardassian bio-technology and gives a requisition number. The Cardassian becomes enraged when he realizes it is a classified item. The Cardassian fears imprisonment if the request is traced to him. It is tied to the dreaded Obsidian Order.

Odo says this branch of the Cardassian secret police is better at what they do than the Romulan Tal Shiar. One mystery leads to another. Although Dr. Bashir first thought the device in Garak's head was for punishment, that's clearly not the case. Garak wants another one.

Julian discovers that Garak regained consciousness and left the infirmary. Bashir goes to Garak's quarters. The doctor informs him Quark won't come through with the merchandise and Garak is experiencing deterioration of his cranial nerve cluster.

Bashir reveals that he knows about the implant. Garak is amused that the doctor thinks it's a punishment device, even though that's what it turns out to be.

Garak says it was given to him by Enabran Tain, the head of the Obsidian Order. It was put there to produce natural endorphins if Garak is tortured. It makes him immune to pain.

Garak hates living on the space station so much that he began to activate the implant. Finally he left it on all the time. It was never intended for such prolonged use and is wearing out.

Garak's body is dependent on the endorphins generated by the implant. He is addicted to it.

This interesting notion could work. Endorphins produced by the human body during strenuous activity enable a person to feel better, such as when a runner gets their "second wind." When someone exercises in the morning, one reason they feel good afterwards is the release of endorphins by the strenuous activity.

The endorphins are chemically similar to opiates. If endorphin production could be artificially stimulated without strenuous physical activity, a person could develop an addiction.

To test Bashir's loyalty and friendship, Garak tells him that he was exiled because he blew up a Cardassian transport holding 97 escaped Bajoran stowaways. He says he used to be a highly feared and respected Gul in the Obsidian Order. Garak is now a war criminal.

This shocking revelation alters the perception of Garak. He later changes the story. By the time the episode concludes, the viewer wonders what is true. The only certainty is that he was in the Obsidian Order. Enabran Tain confirms this.

Bashir decides to shut off the implant and help Garak through withdrawal. During this time Garak is unconscious.

Odo wants to interrogate Garak when he learns Garak claims to have been in the Obsidian Order. The Security Chief insists Garak be awakened for interrogation.

Dr. Bashir refuses. Odo wouldn't have learned anything even though he has several unsolved homicides from the Cardassian period he believes were the work of the Obsidian Order.

Dr. Bashir remains with Garak around the clock. The doctor sees something in Garak that fascinates him. Julian remains loyal even after Garak admits to having committed a war crime.

Garak may have made the statement to test Dr. Bashir. Garak has been shown to be very manipulative in "Cardassians" and "The Wire."

Garak wakes in pain and anger. The implant no longer supplies endorphins to make him feel well. He rages, saying he was stripped of his rank and exiled because he allowed five Bajoran children to go free. Cardassian rules dictated he execute the children.

Garak attacks Dr. Bashir then has another seizure and falls unconscious. Julian determines that toxins are gathering in Garak's lymphatic system. He cannot operate on the station with the limited information he has of Cardassian physiology.

Garak tells a third story of his exile. This time he claims he had a close friend named Elam. Both were picked by Enabran Tain to join the Obsidian Order.

When Bajoran prisoners escaped, rumors implicated someone in the order. Garak planted evidence to implicate Elam. Elam had already implicated Garak. Garak was exiled. He feels shame for abandoning his friend and asks Bashir to forgive him.

So many games. So many conflicting stories. Which are true? The viewer discovers for certain that one of them is untrue. Dr. Bashir takes a runabout to Cardassia Prime to meet with Enabran Tain, Garak's former mentor. Tain has been expecting him and agrees to give Bashir the information he needs to save Garak's lymphatic system.

Enabran Tain helps because he doesn't want Garak to die, yet. He wants him to live a long, miserable life, but doesn't state why.

Tain reveals that Elam is Garak's first name. Garak was well known for telling lies.

Garak responds to the treatment and soon joins Bashir at lunch. He isn't interested in dwelling on recent events. He says Odo has a silly notion that he was once in the Obsidian Order.

Garak has another Cardassian novel for Dr. Bashir to read. It's called MEDITA-TIONS ON A CRIMSON SHADOW. It takes place in the future when Cardassia and the Klingon Empire are at war.

So who is the real Garak? He's a man who never met a lie he didn't like. He mixes lies and truths until they become intertwined.

Garak got the implant in the Obsidian Order. Enabran Tain admitted that. What did Garak do to earn Tain's undying enmity? Garak told three conflicting stories, branding himself a war criminal, a man of compassion condemned by Cardassians or a man framed for helping Bajorans. Are any of these stories true?

This episode doesn't offer Bajoran records to investigate Garak. If he was a Gul serving on Bajor, Major Kira would know. She was in the Bajoran underground and knew many things about her Cardassian slave masters. She isn't consulted.

That she isn't bothered by his presence indicates she doesn't know anything negative about him. Had Garak blown up a transport killing 97 escaped Bajoran prisoners, she'd have known. We can discount that story.

This leaves the story about allowing five Bajoran children to go free. There is nothing to support this story except the lingering enmity of Enabran Tain. There could be other reasons Tain hates Garak.

In "Profit And Loss" it is stated that Garak would have to do a lot more than assassinate a few rogue Cardassians to get back into the good graces of Central Command. Garak's misdeeds loom large in the eyes of his fellow Cardassians. The story of rescuing five children under the age of 15 is sentimental enough to be typical of an inveterate liar such as Garak.

So what is the truth? If he did something Cardassian Central Command despises him for then Garak certainly can't be all bad. He was once in the Obsidian Order, the feared Cardassian Secret Police. If Garak commit crimes against Bajorans he wouldn't be allowed to live unmolested on the space station. He even returned to the surface of Bajor without fear in "Cardassians."

This leaves only hints and scraps of information revealing that Garak is more humane than anyone else from the Cardassian Central Command. He helped Bashir and Sisko undermine Gul Dukat and allowed enemies of the Cardassian Central Command to escape.

This episode reveals little more about Garak. His past remains cloaked in mystery.